Discovering the

Franklins

Fleur Blüm is a Melbourne based writer, performer and musician.

Her blog can be found at https://fleurblum.com/blog

Other works:
Sophie's Path: A choose your own romance adventure
2018

Discovering the Franklins

Fleur Blüm

First edition February 2019

Copyright © 2019 Fleur Blüm
ISBN 978-0-6483654-1-9

Editor: Annie Seaton
Cover Design: Charmaine Ross

Published by Fleur Blüm, Melbourne, Australia

To all the sisters out there

1.

To be or not to be Mrs. Henry Francis McCann

2016

On the night of the third anniversary of her first date with Henry McCann, Sarah Franklin arranged for them to have dinner at a swanky restaurant in South Bank, in the heart of Melbourne's CBD. The reviews said it did the best surf and turf in the city; being Henry's favourite food she hoped he would appreciate her choice.

Sarah had been thinking about their relationship and it needed some work. Mostly Henry took her for granted, but she also knew it wasn't all his fault.

The restaurant was on the second floor of a small shopping centre overlooking the Yarra River. Across the water was the historic train station at Flinders Street, an iconic landmark of Melbourne.

She was seated on the balcony, but the tall gas heater next to her ensured the chill off the water didn't reach her. It was a mild evening in April and the cold weather wasn't far off, Sarah glanced at her watch, just after seven. She took a deep breath and rolled her shoulders back.

Henry was never on time, especially when he had to come straight from work. She didn't know what he did day-to-day, he told her very little about it, but he did name drop the large corporations he consulted with. He was always late home; she thought he worked too hard, but he insisted he had to.

Getting Friday off her nursing roster at the hospital had been a struggle, but she'd had plenty of time to request the leave.

By twenty past seven Henry was making his way through the busy restaurant towards her. His suit was navy-blue suit with subtle pale blue pinstripes and an expensive shirt. With cufflinks, matched the pinstripes.

Henry was hot; over six feet tall with broad shoulders and narrow hips, he was muscular under his tailored suit.

'You have to look as good as the men you're advising, and it's just not done to wear an off the shelf suit with them,' he'd said.

He wore his stark black hair reasonably long and slicked down and was always clean-shaven. It accentuated the strong line of his jaw, and made his aquiline nose look more severe.

'Sorry, babe. I got caught on a conference call to Perth, they didn't realise the time difference. I tried to get here as quick as I could.' His cheeks were flushed, and he radiated heat as she stood to kiss him hello. He must have run part of the way.

'That's okay. I knew you'd be late.'

Even though I was on time, as usual, she thought.

He sat down opposite her and flipped open the drinks list. 'Shall we just get a bottle? Maybe red, to go with the steaks?'

'Sounds fine. You pick.'

Henry insisted on having a good understanding of which were the best wines, purely to impress clients he said, but Sarah knew he just liked having the finer things in life.

'Good evening, have you had a chance to decide what you'd like to drink?' a waiter said, she jumped at his sudden appearance beside her as her attention was so focussed on Henry.

Henry ordered a hundred dollar bottle of red wine from the middle of the wine list.

'I'm sorry I've been so caught up lately. I'm glad we have this opportunity to spend time with each other.' He poured her wine and didn't meet her eye.

'It's alright, for now.'

'It won't be so hectic soon, once the FBT end of year reporting stuff is all sorted I'll be able to focus on you.'

She'd heard that before.

There's always something, she thought.

*   *   *

'Shall we have dessert here? Or do you fancy a walk along the river first?' he asked after the waiter had cleared away their dishes.

'I don't mind, I guess a walk would be nice.' Sarah's suspicions were aroused immediately; Henry had never been one for taking in the view, or for going for a stroll, everything had to have a reason, a purpose.

Cool air flowed over her face as they stepped through the sliding glass doors onto the river front walkway. It had been built up from blue stones and offered a very civilized promenade all the way down to the casino. Henry took her hand and placed it into the crook of his elbow; an unusual gesture which added to Sarah's unease.

Something is going on, she thought, if he's going to ask me for a favour he might have picked the wrong night for it.

*   *   *

Sarah couldn't walk fast in her heels, and Henry had to reduce his stride so she could keep up. The ring was burning a hole in his pocket.

We're in no hurry, he told himself.

He'd been late because he'd lost the ring. When it wasn't in his pocket, he'd panicked and thrown everything on his desk on the floor, emptied out his pockets. He'd worked up a sweat searching before he remembered he gave it to his secretary for safekeeping.

Sarah was talking next to him about the state of the potted vegetable garden they were growing at home. He had a brown thumb at the best of times and even the simple task of watering the plants in the morning slipped his mind.

'I'm sorry, babe, it's just not on my radar. Maybe I'll put a note on the back of the front door. 'Have you watered the plants today, dumb dumb?'' He laughed.

'That might help.' She rested her head briefly on his shoulder.

They had followed the promenade along the length of the river and were approaching the casino. Here a row of thin rectangular towers, referred to as the Gas Brigade, shot balls of flame into the air above them at intervals. Henry loved the unique combination of light, heat and sound they produced.

'Let's stay till they go off.' It was nearly nine and he thought they went on the hour.

'You must have been a pyromaniac in a past life,' she said.

'Maybe.' He put his hand into his pocket, ran his fingers over the velvety box, checking for the hundredth time the ring was still there.

Even though he knew they were coming, the first massive burst of flame caught him off guard. He flinched against Sarah's side, and hoped she didn't notice. He indulged himself watching the fireballs for five blasts before pulling away from her.

He held her shoulders and gently turned her around to face him. They were standing with their profiles to the pillars of flame and he dropped down onto one knee.

'Oh, my God. Henry! What are you doing?' Sarah squealed.

'What does it look like I'm doing?' he said, grinning.

She stamped her feet with glee. 'You have to do it properly.'

'Will you, Sarah Ellen Franklin, do me the honour of becoming my wife?'

'Yes! Yes, of course, yes.'

He held open the black velvet ring box and she took the ring out and slid it on.

'You know I'm not changing my name, right?'

He pouted in mock sadness. 'You won't be Mrs Henry Francis McCann?'

'No. But I'll marry you.'

'Well, I guess that's alright then.'

He stood up and kissed her. He pressed his lips into hers and breathed in the scent of her skin and excitement. Her remembered the first time they'd kissed and the scent of grass and summer then. They kissed for a very long time before he stepped back. The small crowd around them applauded, and he turned to bow theatrically. Sarah giggled.

I hope's this puts end to the 'where is this going' conversation. I'm getting sick of reassuring her, he thought as they walked back to the train station.

2.

The Ring

'Isn't it beautiful?' Sarah said, holding her hand up and wriggling her fingers at her sister. The ring sat on her fourth finger, a fat diamond surrounded by little blue stones, sapphires probably, and a white gold setting. Katie thought it looked like silver, but Henry wouldn't have bought silver.

'You've shown me like five times since you got here.' Katie had been excited for her sister the first two times, then slightly bored, and now was getting annoyed. Katie turned to look out the kitchen window at the grey clouds overhead. Typical of Melbourne it had been threatening rain for days but had yet to produce any.

'Didn't you say you were gonna break up with him last time you were here?'

'Well, yeah, but that was before he did this.' Sarah stared at down at her ring and fiddled with it.

'What's changed though? I mean, really?'

'He's shown he's serious.'

'As far as I can see, he's made a 'grand romantic gesture', it doesn't make him a better boyfriend. And it certainly doesn't demonstrate he's husband material.'

'Don't you get it? He's made a commitment. He's taken the step I needed to make it all worthwhile. The nights when he's working and the constantly being late for our date nights. I mean if he's really serious about us then those things don't matter do they?' Sarah said.

Katie sniffed and rubbed her hands across the fabric of her jeans. 'He's your boyfriend – sorry, fiancé – so you know best.'

'Yes, I do.'

Katie took a sip of her coffee. The two sisters were sitting in her kitchen at the battered formica table in the share house where Katie lived. Sarah disapproved of the situation. Katie hadn't worked out if it was because two of her housemates were students, or some sort of dig about her being single.

'Is he going to help with any of the wedding planning? Have you set a date yet?' Katie had little interest in the wedding but Sarah seemed set on talking about herself.

'We've been riding the high of the actual proposal.'

You have you mean, Katie thought, and Henry is back to being completely self-interested now he's bought himself some time. 'Sounds good.'

Katie's last relationship, with Ella, had ended after only a couple of months. They'd met at a gay night in one of the bars in Smith St, in the inner north of Melbourne. It had been going well, they had lots of mutual interests, Ella followed the football too which helped. She wasn't particularly into fitness, which was fine, except Katie thought it had contributed to their breakup. As a sports physiotherapist in her first year out of university she was very enthusiastic about it. It was hard not to try to correct Ella or encourage her to get active.

'You can't control people.' Ella had said, crying. Katie was completely caught by surprise.

'What do you mean?'

'You know what I mean.'

Katie had known, but she didn't want to admit it had led to another breakup.

'I'm gonna go. Let's not try to be friends.' Ella had picked up her bag and left. Katie sat in her lounge room and stared into space. When her housemates came home later she could barely manage to speak.

And now, less than a fortnight later, she was watching her sister flaunt her newfound relationship bliss.

Am I mad at her because I think the relationship is doomed? Or just because I'm jealous? she thought as Sarah spoke.

'What do you think?' Sarah asked.

'Sorry. Miles away.'

'Typical. I'm trying to share a moment with you and you're making it all about you again.'

'I'm not doing it on purpose. It's just, I've had such bad luck with relationships and you're here with your ring. Even if I did manage to find someone who would stay with me long enough to get married, I can't.'

Sarah's frown deepened. 'I'm sorry. It's shit that, by a simple chance of birth or whatever it is, my relationship is socially acceptable and yours is… well, it kind of isn't… I don't mean it like that.'

Katie looked out the window again, hoping Sarah would drop the subject.

'I just mean it's pathetic in this day and age we're still looking at gays like they're somehow flawed. It's not fair. I'm sorry if I've been insensitive,' Sarah said.

Katie hadn't expected it. 'I… thank you.'

'You'll find your Henry. You're loyal, strong, caring-'

'I'm not a dog.' Katie laughed.

'I'm trying to be nice, you idiot.' Sarah reached her hand across the table and squeezed her sister's forearm.

'I know… tell me again how he did it? Did he kneel and everything?' Katie wanted to get the topic off herself; her sister's new interest in her emotional well-being made her uncomfortable.

3.

The Tree Over the River

1996

'Stop following me,' Sarah said.

'No! I wanna go on the rope swing too!' Katie said.

The two girls made their way towards the river, Sarah, the oldest, ran ahead.

'You're too little to go on the rope swing. It's only for big girls like me.' Sarah puffed out her chest as she spoke. She'd reached the bank where the branches of a gum tree hung over the water. Someone had tied a fat rope around the branch. The rope had two large knots about halfway down its length, just below them a piece of wood was tied on; worn smooth from hands and bums over many summers. The end of the rope looped around the stump of another branch sticking out of the main tree trunk.

Sarah grabbed the rope and pulled it back up the hill. A rut about fifteen centimetres deep ran from the top of the bank down to the river's edge underneath the path of the rope swing. Sarah's legs weren't long enough for her to sit on the wooden seat, so she hooked her arms over it, backed up three more steps and launched herself towards the water.

The wind rushed past her ears; her hair streamed behind her and her T-shirt flapped on her back. She'd done this before, her dad had brought her there last summer. As the felt the rope reach the top of its arc, she let the seat go. She pedalled her legs in the air until she hit the water.

The water was icy cold, but the flow of the river here was slow. She gasped as she breached the surface of the brown muddy river and squealed with surprise.

'Why didn't you wait for me?' Katie stood on the top of the hill looking down at the water her arms crossed over her chest. Last year their dad had insisted she was too young to go on the swing. Sarah was glad it was still her special thing. Now Katie was at school, and with all the trouble with the divorce, she worried Dad would change his mind and she'd have to share the rope swing.

She shivered in the water and doggy-paddled back to the shore. The river mud squelched between her toes as she clambered out. It was her least favourite part. Dad hadn't come around the bend yet, so Sarah decided she would go once more before he got there.

'Get out of the way. I told you, you're too little.'
Sarah pushed Katie aside as she dragged the wet rope
back up the bank to the launch spot.

'I am not. I hate you.'

As Sarah wrapped her arms around the weathered
plank of wood and prepared to launch herself and had
taken only two steps forward when she felt the weight
of her little sister jumping onto her back. The rope
wobbled with the extra weight and Sarah's grip on the
wood slipped.

They were two metres from the launch spot, still
over the dusty ochre earth when they fell heavily into
the furrowed dirt. Sarah landed directly on top of her
sister, who started to wail.

'What's going on here?' Dad jogged towards them.
'Ah fuck, your mum's gonna kill me.' He scrambled
down the bank to where Katie lay, stuck in a hollow in
the ground, apparently unable to move.

Sarah watched, standing a few metres away on the
dusty ground. Her clothes were wet and covered in
mud, her arms hurt where the wood had scratched her,
and her backside ached from the fall. She was getting
cold and she worried she'd be in trouble if Katie was
hurt.

'It wasn't my fault, she jumped on me. I told her she
was too little.'

'You promised you weren't going on the rope, Sarah,' Dad said.

'No, I didn't. You said, 'Promise you won't go in the river' and I didn't say anything.' Sarah shivered violently. Her father didn't look at her.

'I want Mum,' Katie said, her voice wobbled with tears.

'Where does it hurt?' Dad asked.

'All over, everything.'

Dad examined Katie and seemed to find her limbs intact. 'Stick out your tongue.'

'I can't,' she said.

'You must have bitten it when you fell.' He held her small face in his right hand. 'Looks like you'll live. Come on. We better get straight home before you freeze or bleed to death.' Dad scooped Katie up out of the ditch under the rope swing and held out his hand to Sarah. She bent to pick up her thongs and marched off, barefoot, towards the car.

She reached it well ahead of her dad and sister and sat down on the narrow ledge at the back to wait for them. Her dad had a big green Land Rover, for going camping, he said. He hadn't taken them yet, but he'd promised they'd go in the school holidays. The car always smelled of petrol and grass from when he put his tools in there for work. From outside she could almost smell it.

It seemed like a very long time before the other two came out of the trees and joined her.

'I don't think we need to tell Mum what happened, do you?' Dad directed the question at both girls. Katie snuggled into his arms like a baby, and Sarah hated her.

'What about my clothes. They're all muddy. You'll have to wash them,' she said.

Dad spoke through clenched his teeth. 'We'll see to that.'

4.

The Next Day

By the next morning Katie's tongue was apparently so sore she refused to speak. Sarah was not speaking to her father either. When he'd washed her clothes Dad had put them in with his underpants.

'I can't wear them now. They've got your poo all over them,' she said.

'What? My boxers don't have poo on them. Your clothes are clean, Sarah, you put them back on right now.'

Sarah stood in her pyjamas, her sister watching silently, and shook her head.

'I'm going to count to three…'

Sarah walked past her father and into the kitchen. The kitchen cabinets were dirty white and the benchtops were a horrible orange like the colour you'd get if you squeezed a rotten peach. She stood next to the fridge, waiting.

'You aren't getting breakfast until you've put your clothes on. There's nothing wrong with them, and if you won't wear your clothes, Mum will be suspicious and then I'll get in trouble.' Dad followed her in.

'Good, I want you to be in trouble. I hate you,' Sarah said.

Her dad ran his hand over his face. 'I'm sorry you hate me. I love you, I will love you no matter what. But you aren't getting breakfast until you're wearing proper clothes.'

'You can't starve me. I know my rights.'

He made a noise in his throat like a groan. 'You're right. I can't starve you. You can have one piece of toast with no butter or jam on it. If you want spread, you can put your clothes on.'

Sarah threw up her hands. 'Fine.'

Her sister was now hovering in the doorway of the kitchen.

'You want something to eat kiddo? Maybe, uh, a nice warm Milo? So you don't have to chew.'

Of course she gets warm Milo for breakfast, Sarah thought, walking back to her room where she dragged her pyjamas off and put her clothes back on. She was still suspicious they had poo on them, but her tummy grumbled and reminded her that toast without anything on it was too gross to endure.

Discovering the Franklins

Katie was sitting at the kitchen table when Sarah came back in. Graham lived in a share house since he'd moved out of the house he'd shared with their mum. He said he couldn't afford to rent the whole place to himself. His housemate, Chris, was divorced too, a pale man who Sarah didn't really like. He smelled funny, like B.O. and cigarettes and his clothes had holes in them.

Chris walked out into the kitchen, fixing himself an instant coffee; he didn't talk. Dad warmed some milk in the microwave and added milo to it.

'See, this is the only way to get it to be all nice and smooth,' he said as he stirred the third teaspoon into the mug. 'Don't look at me like that,' he added looking at Chris. 'She has a sore mouth.'

Chris raised his eyebrows. 'I didn't say anything.'

'Here you go. I could make you a Milo too if you're going to be good?' Dad looked at Sarah.

She didn't reply

'Careful, if it's too hot just blow on it, okay?' he said to Katie.

Dad moved over to where she sat. Everything seemed so unfair.

'You okay, monkey?' he asked.

'I wish you and Mum still liked each other.'

25

'I know you do, baby. I do too, but you remember what it was like when we tried to pretend? And we were both sad and cranky all the time?'

'But can't you just be not sad and cranky?'

'Have you ever tried to not be cranky?' He smiled.

'Yes. I tried today but I'm still mad at Katie for jumping on me.'

'I know you didn't mean to hurt her. She shouldn't have jumped on you, but she's only little. She'll know for next time eh?'

Chris was leaning on the bench near the sink, his steaming cup in his hands. Dad put two slices of bread into the white metal toaster and took out the Nutella.

He must be trying to make up for giving Katie Milc, Sarah thought.

'I'm sorry I squashed you. I didn't mean to,' she said.

'I dow.' Katie replied around her inflamed tongue.

5.

Have you set a date?

2016

'You're home late.' Sarah was already in bed this time. Henry was wearing his grey suit today with a vest and a blue shirt. His tie was already in his hand. He had a submission for one of his big clients looming. Home after ten every night this week and gone before seven each morning.

'Yeah, it's been hectic.' He leaned over the bed to kiss her forehead.

'It's not sustainable you know, they can't work you this hard forever.'

'I know, babe, the submission will be in soon and then I'll be able to take a couple of days off. Maybe we can go down to Phillip Island or something. A little break.'

'That sounds nice.' Sarah rolled over and went to sleep.

*　　　*　　　*

She didn't feel Henry get into the bed but woke to his alarm. She didn't have to work until three p.m., so she stayed in bed while he went about his morning routine.

'Have a good day,' she called.

'You too.' He pulled the door shut behind him.

Their apartment was on the first floor in a set of four in Clifton Hill, a suburb in the north close to the city but not as trendy as neighbouring Fitzroy. It felt very empty as she snuggled back down into the covers. The August morning was chilly; Henry didn't like to put the heater on unless it was really cold and his definition of really cold differed to hers.

Sarah shivered and flicked back the covers. It would be no use trying to get back to sleep now. She flicked on the central heating and cranked it up to twenty-five degrees.

I'll put it back down once it's taken the edge off, she thought.

Henry had left his blue shirt crumpled in a heap on the bathroom floor when he came in last night, she picked it up. It gave off a waft of scent as she picked it up, she lifted it to her face. Perfume. Strong women's perfume.

Maybe the client's secretary wears a lot of perfume, I've certainly met my fair share of uptight business ladies who reek, she thought.

Sarah put on a load of washing, swept the floors, and made herself a coffee with the machine the Henry had bought.

He hardly used it, even on weekends when he was at home he tended to go out to a café rather than make coffee. Sometimes Sarah wondered how two people with such obviously different values had ever ended up together, but that led to unpleasant thoughts. Like whether she really wanted to be with Henry.

Of course, she loved him; stable, employed, kind to wait staff, and she'd never suspected him of cheating, unless she counted being married to his work. His friends were all very cool, up and coming types with high-flying jobs like he had. Their partners were much more high maintenance than her. Acrylic nails, fake tans, new hairstyles every six months. They all seemed to have Barbie doll figures, long legs and big boobs. Her own figure was boyish in comparison. Sure, she had nice legs, but no bum or boobs to speak of. Her long hair fell almost to her waist, a boring middle brown and dead straight. It wouldn't hold any curl or volume, so she usually just tied it back in a low ponytail.

She'd tried dyeing it once.

29

'What did you do that to your hair for?' Henry had said when he saw it.

'You don't think the highlights suit me?'

'No. Did you pay someone to do that?' He'd almost laughed at her.

'Yeah, one of the girls at work recommended someone.' Her cheeks had flushed, and she'd felt ashamed.

'Your hair is gorgeous. Don't I always say so? Why would you mess with it?' He drew her into a hug.

She rested her hair against his broad chest. 'I thought you'd like it.'

'Well, I like the real you. I don't want a Barbie on my arm for parties. Don't try to be something you're not, babe. Just be you.'

She'd remembered why she loved him then; he was a straight talker: sometimes hurtful, and sometimes nice. Then there were times, like this one, it seemed to be both.

She had dyed her hair back to its normal colour by the end of the week and she'd never tried to be like those other women again.

*   *   *

That afternoon Sarah went to work at the large public hospital in Fitzroy where she was a nurse. She could have walked to work if she wanted but she was usually running late and drove.

'Hey love, how's tricks?' her work friend Ned asked.

'Fine. You know.'

'That good?'

'No, it's fine, really. It's just Henry's been working really a lot lately, and I had all these ideas about the wedding I wanted to run by him.'

'Have you set a date then?' Ned asked.

'No. We haven't even been able to sit down and agree on how soon we should do this. He keeps saying there's no hurry, but if we want to have a big wedding we'll need to get onto the waiting lists for venues and I have no idea how long those things take, you know?'

'Yeah, I know.'

'I guess it doesn't really matter.' Sarah shrugged and tried to get on with her work, but the nugget of sadness in her throat stayed there all day.

6.

A nice day for a white wedding

2017

Sarah sat at home waiting for Henry.

Again. They were supposed to be meeting with the wedding planner to go over the final details before the rehearsal next Saturday. It was only a week until the wedding after that.

Sarah had planned almost all of it alone. After pleading and negotiating with Henry over the date for nearly a year, he had finally agreed to September. She had less than six months to get everything ready. He'd been working all the time, as usual. On a good week, he was only in the office from eight until six, including weekends, on a bad week he only came home to sleep.

It didn't seem to bother him he had nothing outside of his work and she'd given up trying to get him to have a hobby, or take an interest in the plants, or anything she did. The only thing he seemed interested in was the gym, and they had one in the building he worked in.

The wedding planning had highlighted how lonely she felt in the relationship. Once they were married, once these couple of big projects were finished, surely things would be better.

'We're supposed to be meeting Greta. As it is we're going to be 20min late. Where are you?' She texted him, her fingers drummed on the surface of the glass coffee table as she waited for a reply.

'I need to finish some stuff before I can leave. Why don't you go? I trust you have everything under control.'

'Typical,' she said out loud. She didn't reply to the message.

They were meeting Greta, the wedding planner, at the venue; a country estate about an hour to the south-east of Melbourne. They had a vineyard and produced their own wine, but they also had a restaurant, cellar door, and hosted weddings. More expensive than she'd wanted, but Henry had insisted they had the best. And he knew a guy who knew the owner, it was a networking opportunity he couldn't pass up.

He'd never even managed to see it in person. The few times she'd been to set things up he said he would come, but something had come up every time. She shook her head. She considered asking if he'd be available on the wedding day or whether he would have to finish something for work and keep all their guests waiting. She picked up her phone to text him and she gripped it so hard her fingers hurt. She unclenched her jaw and her hand and stood up.

She got into her car, a little white VW she'd bought second hand about four years ago, about to reverse of out the carpark underneath their little apartment. No good getting angry with him when he wasn't around, he would say she was being unfair, and if they had a fight they should do it in person, and in private.

'I wonder when that will be,' she said to herself. She put her phone into the dashboard holder and programmed in the address of the wedding venue. She'd already let the planner know she'd be late and Henry wouldn't be there.

She called Katie; she didn't have football till tomorrow and might be up for a road trip.

'Yeah?' Katie answered.

'It's me.'

'I know.'

'I'm going to the Yarra Valley for final wedding stuff. Henry's ditched me for work. Wanna come?'

Katie sighed. 'Alright.'

'I'll be there in two minutes.'

'Geez, don't give me any notice...see you soon then.'

Discovering the Franklins

*   *   *

The share house Katie lived in was a sprawling old house in the middle of new flats and renovated heritage houses. Sarah marvelled the landlord hadn't been bought out and the place bulldozed. There were no parking spots, so she double parked and honked.

Katie will hate that, she thought with a little grin, so worried about what the neighbours think.

A wooden veranda ran across the front of the house; all the floor boards were worn grey and were in need of polishing and staining. Some previous tenant had scrounged a vinyl covered three-seater lounge that now lived on the veranda. The cushions were cracked and peeling, and when Sarah had sat there last summer, she'd come away with her legs and arms covered in vinyl flakes where her skin had touched it.

She honked again.

*   *   *

Katie opened the front door and gave her sister the finger before pulling the door shut and running out to the car, holding her shoes and socks in her hands.

'You've got toothpaste on your face.' Sarah reached out to rub it off.

Katie turned away and flipped down the sun-visor to look in the mirror as Sarah pulled out onto the road. 'Thanks.'

They were quiet for a while as Katie put on her shoes and ran her fingers through her short-cropped hair.

'What's his excuse this time?' Katie asked.

'Work.'

'It's Saturday.'

'Yeah.'

Katie sighed.

'Did I pull you away from anything?' Sarah asked after a while.

'Not really. Thought about going to Ikea but I don't really have any money so, you probably saved me at least a hundred bucks.'

They were quiet again and Katie opened the glovebox and flipped through the CDs. Most of them were copies and didn't have labels, she would never understand the system Sarah used.

'Does he get this is important?' Katie said.

'I…' Sarah sniffed. 'I think he does, but it doesn't translate to his behaviour. I guess I've let him get away with it for our whole relationship and now he doesn't think there are any consequences.'

Sarah turned up the music. Katie understood the subject was closed and stared out the window as the trees whipped by beside the freeway.

*   *   *

Discovering the Franklins

The driveway into the venue was long and covered in dusty ochre gravel. The sound of the tiny stones against the sides of the car sounded like rain. The sun was out, and the air was clear to the horizon in all directions: a beautiful place to be married. The early September sun was still weak, and Katie shivered a little in her T-shirt and jeans when she stepped out of the car.

Greta was already waiting for them, wearing a form fitting navy-blue skirt and matching blazer, with beige stilettos. Her dyed blond hair fell in gorgeous curls around her face and her make-up was impeccable as usual. The light breeze blew a lock of hair across her eyes and she reached up a French-manicured hand to tuck it behind her ear.

'Sorry we're late. You remember my sister, Katie?'

'Of course.' Greta held out her hand to both before trotting inside. The sisters followed her.

Greta went through her list of items: the flowers, the chairs, the table settings, catering. Katie wasn't really listening, but Sarah seemed to be relaxing a little with each item discussed.

'Are we doing any tasting today?' Katie asked.

'Uh, no, that's all been done.' Greta faltered a little as she had to interrupt her stream to answer.

'Right.' Katie's belly rumbled, she'd only had time to roll out of bed before Sarah honked outside.

'We'll get something before we go. You have to try their poached salmon, it's so good,' Sarah said quietly as Greta continued.

Once they'd been through everything on Greta's list, and been assured everything was on track the sisters were left to themselves in the vast restaurant. Open plan and mostly clean white lines, floor to ceiling windows looked out over the vineyards and rolling hills.

Katie ordered the salmon, as instructed, and Sarah had a steak. Katie watched her sister constantly checking her phone, probably hoping for something from Henry.

*   *   *

'Have you heard from Henry?' Katie asked when they were back on the road, the late afternoon sun slanting over the vineyards as they made their way back to the freeway.

'He said he'd call as soon as he finished, but that was this morning before we set off.'

'You're not worried what he's getting up to?'

'No. I know he's not lying to me. The problem has never been lying to me. The problem is not being important. Getting married was supposed to fix that.' Sarah's lip began to tremble.

'Hey, I'm sorry, I didn't mean to upset you.'

'You aren't the one who's at work instead of preparing for our wedding.'

'I'm sorry,' Katie said.

'I know.'

'I'm sure it's just a hump, he'll finish this, project or whatever, and then he'll be there for you more.'

'Maybe.'

Katie waited for her sister to say more, but she didn't.

*　　*　　*

Sarah dropped Katie off and when she pulled into her apartment car park, she noticed Henry's pushbike chained up at the front of their space.

'I'm home,' she called as she entered the apartment. The kitchen and lounge were both empty. She went into the bedroom to put down her handbag and she heard the shower running.

'Hi babe!' she said, louder this time so he'd hear her over the water. He didn't respond.

She took off her shoes and lay down on the bed. She picked up her book but didn't open it.

'I didn't hear you come in,' Henry said, his hand holding the towel around his waist closed.

'I called out. How was work?'

'The usual.' Henry lay down on the bed next to her.

'Greta said everything's in place,' she said.

'Good.'

'Babe. Look at me.'

Henry turned to face her. 'I said good.'

'Is it always going to be like this?'

'Like what?'

'Like I'm on my own. Like you're married to your work instead of me. This morning I thought 'is he even going to come to the wedding? He's missed just about everything else.''

'That's not fair. I've been working hard so we can afford this fucking wedding and you're criticising me?'

'I didn't want it to be expensive! That was all your idea. I went along with it because I made so many other decisions I thought I should let you have some.' As Sarah sat up, propped on one elbow, her chest constricted with anger.

'You never asked for it, but you would have complained forever if I'd been tight.'

'Hello? It's me, Sarah Franklin, the least fancy person ever. I would have been happy with twenty people in the registry office and a barbeque afterwards.'

'Sure you would have.' He turned away, staring at the ceiling.

'This pageantry is all for your benefit. So you can invite your work associates and make a good impression. I suppose I should know you'll be there because you've invited the boss and you wouldn't let him down. You only let me down.'

'I'm sorry you had to go alone.'

'I took Katie.'

'Your dyke sister?'

'Don't call her that.'

'Why not? It's what she is,' he said.

Sarah clenched her teeth. 'Why are you being such an arsehole?'

'I'd like a bit of gratitude for the fact my salary affords us this house.'

'I pay my way.'

'Not half, babe, not nearly half. We would be living in a dive like your sister if we paid the rent you could afford.'

She turned back to face him, trying not to look at his bare chest. 'All I'm hearing is appearances are more important to you than being a good boyfriend. I thought when you proposed things would change. I thought it meant I was important.'

'You are important!'

'I can count on one hand the number of waking hours we've spent together this week. That's not a boyfriend. It's certainly not a husband.'

'What do you want me to do about it?'

'Stop taking on so much work. Be here with me, at least at the weekends. We don't see each other, and I feel like I'm in this alone.'

'You're not.' Henry reached out and took her hand. When she felt his touch, she started to cry. He pulled her down to him and held her to his chest, firm and comforting. The smell of him, clean from the shower and still slightly damp, sent that old thrill down to her groin.

She tilted her head up and kissed him. Softly at first, but as her arousal built she became more insistent, pushing her lips against his, relishing the baby soft skin of his face.

'Sorry babe, I'm wrecked. Maybe in the morning.' He pushed her away.

Her stomach clenched in anger. 'I'm staying with Katie tonight.'

'What? Why?'

'You need your rest.' She picked up her shoes and handbag and stormed back out of the apartment.

7.

Dear Diary

2006

Sarah wrote in her journal every day. It was how she processed what had happened that day at school. She was class captain and she had plenty of friends, but she had this gnawing feeling things weren't quite right.

She kept her current journal with her most of the time and her old ones in a shoebox under her bed. Katie had seen her writing in them but had never tried to read them as far as she knew. If she caught her sister snooping around in them there would be trouble.

She stared at her year eleven biology homework trying to make sense of the diagram of a dissected frog. They'd had to cut them down the middle, pin their chest cavities open and pull out their organs. Sarah had only been able to do it by keeping her mind firmly focused on the task and not thinking about what the poor frog was like before it had died.

Around her, the other students had been carrying on, taunting each other with little bits of frog held with long stainless-steel tweezers and flung across the tables. Sarah couldn't watch them. She'd put her head down and made her diagram as detailed as she could.

Now, sitting in her bedroom, her blue desk lamp shining down on the white paper, she struggled to translate what she'd put on her diagram into the report she was writing on her laptop.

If I take five minutes to check whether anyone has sent me a message on MSN, that would be okay, she thought. The report wasn't due until Friday, so she had another two nights to work on it. If she really couldn't get it done, she could always tell Miss Greggs she'd accidentally left it at home and would hand it in first thing on Monday. She'd still have the whole weekend to finish it.

Sarah opened MSN messenger; she had no new messages.

Steve said he would give me the details of the party tonight. He promised, she thought. She knew some of the popular kids in year twelve, the year above her, had organized a party at Steve's because his parents were travelling in Europe.

She'd been to parties there before. His parents went away at the same time every year, they said they couldn't handle the winters in Melbourne and preferred the Côte d'Azur.

Who wouldn't prefer that? Sarah had thought when she heard this.

Steve's parents were rich, but not particularly involved in his life. He was the guy who would get you alcohol or weed if you needed it; he had connections. If you didn't have money, he would sometimes ask you to do his assignments for him. But only if you were a good student.

'Dummies have to have cash,' he'd said to Sarah.

'Uh, am I a dummy?'

'No, you're an above average student from what I heard. I mean you do have the disadvantage of being younger, so you haven't done the course work yet, but I'd let you do an English assignment for me if you ever needed any…party favours.'

'I think I'm okay for now, but I'll tell you if I change my mind.' She'd smiled at him like an idiot and hoped he meant it.

Steve was tall, broad-shouldered and was already shaving. 'I could grow a full beard if I wanted. Stupid teachers reckon you have to shave though.'

The dress code didn't extend to his hair, which hung below his shoulders; brown with natural blonde highlights, and a slight curl. He wore it in a ponytail low on the back of his neck.

Sarah pulled out her journal. She knew Steve wouldn't be interested in dating her, she was only in year eleven, and she was skinny and short. Her father was tall, but not her mother. Unfortunately for Sarah, she had inherited most of her mother's genes. She was one hundred and sixty-five centimetres tall, not the shortest person she knew, but she had to stretch to reach the hanging handholds on the train. Her hair was long and brown. Not thick but not thin either. It insisted on hanging straight down no matter what she did. Katie's hair was the same, but somehow it suited her.

Usually Sarah wrote in her journal last thing before going to bed. It helped her fall asleep. She looked at the clock, it was after ten, and she decided to pack away her homework and close her computer. If Steve wanted to invite her to the party, he would, and if not, then she'd have to accept he was out of her league.

She slipped into bed, enjoying the feeling of the sheets sliding over her legs. The late July nights were cold, but she refused to wear pyjama bottoms, it felt too restrictive. Her mother had helped her buy a double bed for her room at the start of the year. She'd had to save up until she could pay for half. She felt so grown up in the big bed.

Her current journal was plain black leather with lined pages inside. She got a thick one so she didn't have to spend her money buying new journals all the time. She held it in her hands and ran them over the cover, the smell of the leather wafting up to her as she did. She had a special journal writing pen too, the one her dad had given her for her birthday a couple of years ago. Back when he still seemed to care what was happening in her life.

'Dear diary,

Steve is so dreamy but I don't think he's into me. I don't know how to make him notice me.'

She went on in this vein for about ten minutes before she moved on to the other girls in her class and then complaining about her sister.

*   *   *

In the morning Katie crept into her sister's room and found her sleeping with her journal lying open beside her. In the half-light streaming in around the curtains, Katie hovered over the bed trying to read last night's entry.

Most mornings Katie snuck in, Sarah was a heavy sleeper and she had to remind herself not to become too bold. The pages lying open talked about Steve, the vacuous pretty boy she was currently obsessed with, Katie skimmed until she got to the part about her.

'Why does Katie want to hang out with me all the time? It's pathetic. I mean doesn't she have her own friends? God. I'm going to tell Mum she can't come with me to the library on the weekend. I need to study with Jenna and having Katie there means we can't talk about the important stuff.'

Sarah constantly complained about having to have her sister hanging around. Katie hated her for it, but she would still rather be with Sarah than alone. She always had trouble making friends and Sarah seemed to do it so easily.

Still, Sarah thought she was so important and impressive, being class captain and having all the other girls wrapped around her little finger. It felt good to know Steve wasn't interested. At least she didn't get her way all the time.

Katie backed away quietly, Sarah had started to stir, and her alarm would be going off any minute. She took a long time to get up in the mornings. Their mother would call her at least seven times before she emerged and went straight into the bathroom. As a result of always sleeping in, Sarah often ate her breakfast on the bus on the way to school. These days she was on to some expensive breakfast bars, which looked more like trumped up biscuits to Katie.

'They're full of fibre,' Sarah said.

Sure they are, Katie thought.

Katie was an early riser, she always woke before her alarm, which was how she'd discovered the perfect way to read Sarah's diary.

Discovering the Franklins

The first time she'd done it, she wanted to borrow a top. They were almost the same size, in spite of the age difference. Two years wasn't really that much anyway. Katie would probably end up being bigger than her sister; she was sportier and already slightly taller.

It was hard, at first, to know what Sarah thought of her without getting really angry. The first day Katie had read something about herself she'd paced up and down in her room for a good twenty minutes before she'd managed to calm herself enough to eat. Mum, Hannah, seemed to have picked up that something had changed between the sisters, but hadn't said anything.

So far, Sarah had been totally oblivious to the entire thing. Katie swore off writing a journal of any sort.

She didn't do much with the information usually; she just liked the power of knowing. Once Steve had called the house phone looking for Sarah, but she'd told him she was out and never passed on the message. Knowing Sarah liked Steve made these small acts of sabotage much more significant.

Katie ate her breakfast— four Weetbix, which she'd sprinkled generously with sugar, strawberries, and milk. Mum was chopping celery which would go into the salads she prepared each morning for school lunches. Katie thought it was a bit much being expected to eat salad all through winter as well, but not enough to make her own lunches.

'Come on Sarah, it's seven forty-five.'

She'll need at least another call, Katie thought. To her surprise Sarah walked through the door to the kitchen already in her school uniform.

'You're up early,' Katie said.

'Fuck you.'

'Don't swear at your sister.' Their mother didn't turn around.

She picked up the kettle and wobbled it. Then refilled it at the tap and put it on to boil. Sarah sat opposite Katie and stared at her Weetbix.

'What's eating you? Haven't heard from Steve lately?' Katie said.

'What makes you think I'm waiting for Steve?'

Katie lowered her voice. 'Isn't there a big party you haven't been invited to?'

'How do you know that?'

'I uh...' Katie had read it in the diary. 'I heard some of the girls at school laughing at you yesterday.' Her cheeks grew hot.

'You liar. You fucking liar.'

'Don't swear,' said Hannah, again.

'How did you hear about the party? No one knows I haven't got an invite. Everyone thinks I'm going, so how do you know?'

'I told you.' Katie was not an accomplished liar.

'The only person I told is my diary...you've read my fucking diary? You bitch! You absolute fucking slut.'

'That's it. You're not going to any parties this weekend, Sarah, since you can't keep your mouth clean. As for you,' her mother turned her stony gaze on Katie. 'Reading Sarah's journal? It's pathetic. I didn't raise you to be a spy and a sneak.'

'You didn't even wait for me to say anything. What if I didn't do it!'

'Did you?' Hannah said. Both sets of eyes were on her now. She couldn't lie under pressure.

'Yeah, alright, I did. It's not that big a deal. I mean really...'

'I'm never speaking to you again. You're a two-faced bitch and I hate you.' Sarah turned and ran out of the room.

Hannah said nothing. The kettle had boiled, and she made a cup of instant coffee, putting an extra spoon of sugar into it.

'You need to think about what you've done. Betraying your sister...I don't know what's gotten into you.' She turned and walked out of the kitchen. Katie listened to her footfalls as she walked to Sarah's bedroom, knocked, and then went in.

'Fuck,' Katie said aloud to the empty kitchen.

8.

You again?

2017

Katie ordered pizza and had just settled down on the lumpy couch to watch T.V. with her housemates when someone knocked on the door.

'That can't be the pizza yet,' she said. She padded to the front door in her socks. She didn't like to wear shoes in the house, but the floorboards were cold under her feet.

Katie opened the door and saw her sister there for the second time in a day. She said nothing.

'Can I come in?' Sarah asked after a long pause.

'Of course, sorry.'

Sarah followed her into the lounge room. 'Can we, uh, talk?' she asked quietly.

Katie nodded to her room, Sarah slumped onto the bed as she swung the door shut.

'I didn't expect to see you again tonight.'

'Yeah. Well.'

Katie waited.

'Is marrying Henry a mistake?' Sarah asked.

'Wow, that's a big question.'

Sarah told her what had happened without crying, but only just, Katie watched her mouth twist itself into weird shapes with the effort.

'And you came over here?'

'Yes.'

'Well, I mean I can't tell you how you feel, I can only say what I see. And I see Henry doesn't really spend much time with you.'

'I thought it would get better.'

'Maybe it will.' Katie didn't believe it.

'If we go through with this wedding, if we spend all that money and nothing changes, I'll feel like an idiot.'

'You're not an idiot.'

'Thanks. But I'd still feel like one.'

Katie shifted back on the bed, leaning her back against the headboard she'd made by gluing fabric and foam to a slab of MDF she found on the side of the road once.

'If you cancel the wedding, would you break up with him?'

'I think I kind of have to, don't you?'

'I dunno, you can do what you like. He'll probably think it's a breakup.'

'I don't know if I want to break up.' Sarah picked at her jeans.

'But...?'

'I don't want to go through with the wedding. I thought he'd be different. You know when he proposed...'

'You can't change who he is. He has to want to change.'

'The more I think about it, the more annoying habits I come up with... like he spends an awful lot of money on shit; he has more pairs of shoes than me, and he's had a different car every year since we've been together,' Sarah said.

'Doesn't he make some ridiculous amount of money?'

'Yeah, but he spends all of it. We couldn't afford to go on a honeymoon because he bought a $10,000 watch.'

'You're not going away after the ceremony?'

'No. Initially he said he couldn't get the time off, but when I looked into where we could go, even just a week at Phillip Island, he got annoyed with my suggestions and finally admitted after the wedding costs, he didn't have any money left.'

'Wow.' Katie was truly surprised, Henry seemed so rich.

'And it was him who insisted on having a massive wedding anyway. I don't know why he's blaming me for having no money left.'

'I'm sorry.' Katie didn't want to put ideas into her sister's head. It was a big decision and even though she thought Henry was a moron, Sarah had to live with the decision.

'Do you want to stay here tonight? I can take the couch.' Katie said.

'If it's alright, I mean we can share the bed.'

Katie grabbed her sister in an awkward hug, Sarah lay limp in her arms. 'It's been a long day. Why don't I get you some wine, and we can watch something? When the pizza comes we'll share it.'

* * *

During the night Sarah lay awake for a long time. The wine had made her sleepy, but as soon as the lights were out she was wide awake. She lay listening to her sister's breathing as it slowed and finally became a light snore.

They hadn't shared a bed since they were small. After their parents' divorce their father had struggled financially. He always tried to get a better deal, flitting from one job to the next. Once he gave up on share-housing, he could only ever afford to live in a one-bedroom granny flat out the back of a property in Eltham. When they stayed with him, the girls would have the bed, and he'd sleep on the couch. They were only ever there on the weekends and it had seemed like an adventure when they were children. By the time Sarah was fourteen, they were fighting so much they could only stay with their dad separately.

She was used to sleeping next to a person, she didn't know what it would feel like to sleep on her own again after years sleeping next to Henry. She'd have to move out, and the idea of going back to sharing seemed so frightening she considered marrying Henry just to avoid it.

But she couldn't marry him. Now she'd finally seen him for who he was; a workaholic, image-obsessed, husk of a man, she could never go back.

When he worked long hours and claimed it would just be for that project and it would be different at the end of the month, she knew he'd accept the next job and it wouldn't be different at all. Every time she came home to find he'd bought some flashy toy, or a package turned up in the mail she had to pick up because he never made it to the post office, she'd be reminded of how she didn't get a honeymoon.

Her thoughts went around and around in her head as she lay next listening to her sister's breathing.

*   *   *

Sarah didn't think she would ever get to sleep but when she woke up in the morning she realised she must have dozed off. Katie was still snoozing, but it the sun was up and Sarah needed to get moving. She was a habitual early riser these days and didn't like to waste the day lying around in bed, even when she'd had a difficult night, and nothing needed to be done.

She dressed quietly and slipped out into the kitchen. No one else got up this early on a Sunday morning, and both the solitude and the early morning sunshine streaming in through the windows made her glad she had this moment alone.

She'd thought it looked like rain last night, but the ground was dry, and the skies were clear. Perhaps the weather approved of her decision.

Sarah made herself a coffee with the stovetop brewer Katie's housemates had. She didn't know if she should use the coffee without asking, but she could easily buy another pack if someone kicked up a stink. Henry hadn't tried to call her during the night. She wouldn't have answered him, but he hadn't even tried.

He probably just went to sleep and hoped I'd calm down ask for forgiveness in the morning, she thought. It was usually how things went. Henry behaved poorly, and then had some reason he thought justified it, and she would apologise for getting upset. He had lots of excuses, but never said he was sorry.

How many things had she said sorry for during their almost five-year relationship? How many times had she given in? Her hand curled tightly around the handle of the coffee mug she held. She took her coffee cup and went out to the beaten-down old couch on the front veranda.

'Hi,' he said when she called him.

'Hi.' She didn't know how to start.

'I hope you've calmed down a bit. It wasn't really fair for you to crack it last night.'

'Calmed down?'

'Yes. It's a bit histrionic to storm out of the house the week before the wedding. I thought you were above Bridezilla bullshit,' he said.

Sarah clenched her teeth and put her coffee on the veranda so she wouldn't spill it from shaking. 'I'm sorry if you felt put out by my emotions, Henry.'

'Apology accepted. When will you be home? I have to go into the office.'

'I'm not coming home.' She couldn't believe she'd said it.

'What do you mean?'

'I mean, I'm not coming home. I'm not going to marry you.'

'What the fuck? You've been planning this solidly for six months.'

'Yes. I have. You have barely helped, except to spend money. I hardly see you and you certainly don't have any time for sex. I've had enough. I'm out.'

'Jesus. You're serious?'

'Yes. I'm serious.'

'You're crazier than I thought.'

'Excuse me?'

'I really don't have time for this.'

Sarah laughed. 'No, of course you don't. You have to get back to the office. I'll call everyone tomorrow to cancel everything. I'll arrange to have my stuff picked up from the apartment in the next week. When it's all gone, I'll let you know where I've left the key.'

'You're a cold-hearted bitch, Sarah. You couldn't have picked a worse time. Work is really hectic and now we'll probably lose most of our deposits – the food, the venue, they'll all want their money.'

'Your first thought is the deposits?' she said. She stood up and started pacing up and down the veranda trying to keep her breathing even.

'Now you've dumped me it's all wasted money, isn't it?'

Sarah could barely speak over the fury constricting her throat. 'I'll let you know when it's all sorted. Have a good life.'

'Yeah, fuck you too.' Henry hung up.

Sarah carefully put her phone onto the veranda in front of the couch and lay down on the flaky imitation leather cushions. She felt a spikey prickle in her eyes, but the tears didn't come. She felt numb, all she could do was keep breathing, steadily in and out.

*　　*　　*

Katie woke up alone. It took her a minute to remember why that felt wrong. She wrapped herself in her black flannelette dressing gown and went to find Sarah. When she saw her lying on the veranda couch, her knees tucked up in the foetal position she knew what had happened.

'You alright?'

'I don't know.'

Katie sat on one of the arms, which creaked in protest, and stroked her sister's hair.

'Now what?' she asked after a while.

'I don't know.'

'You can stay here for a few days if you need to.'

'Thanks.'

She felt helpless. Sarah lay there, not moving, and barely talking. What was she supposed to do?

'Are you hungry?' she asked.

'Not really.'

'Oh. You want another coffee?' She looked at the barely touched cup on the veranda.

'Not really.'

'Are you cold?'

'A bit.'

'Why don't you come inside? I'll put the tele on and you can lie on the couch. No need to do anything, okay?'

They went inside, and Katie put a blanket over her sister. She had a football game at two o'clock in Fitzroy she didn't want to miss, but she couldn't leave Sarah there on her own. She went about her usual Sunday morning routine, occasionally putting her head into the lounge to check on Sarah; but there was no change.

As game time approached, Sarah roused herself.

'I'm going back to sleep, is that alright?'

'Of course. I'm going to a game. Will you be okay here on your own?'

'I'm a grown woman. I'll be fine.' She attempted to smile.

'You'll be alright. Just rest. I'll make you some dinner when I get home, but if you're hungry in the meantime just… eat whatever and we'll sort it out later. I love you.' She hugged her sister where she was on the couch, Sarah did not hug her back, but didn't pull away, and jogged out the door.

9.

Not via text

Katie put Sarah's phone away in her bedside drawer and made sure she didn't look at it. Today wasn't the day for practical things. It was a day for grieving and self-soothing. She brought home chicken and chips from a place near the footy oval in Fitzroy North.

The chips were only slightly sweaty by the time she came in. Sarah was on the couch in her pyjamas, with the T.V. on but it didn't seem like she was paying much attention to it.

'Dinner.' She plonked the packet on the coffee table in front of her sister.

'I know that smell,' Sarah said, struggling to sit upright.

'Break ups call for indulgence. You need a plate?'

'No, I'm alright. Maybe a fork?' Sarah pulled open the bag and the smell of chips and charcoal chicken wafted through the lounge.

They ate in silence as a reality cooking show dragged what should have been ten minutes of material into a full hour. Katie wasn't a fan of watching and eating, but Sarah didn't look like she could do much else.

As the show started the teaser for the next night's show Sarah turned to her. 'Do you know where my phone is?' she asked.

'I hid it. So you wouldn't be tempted to talk to stupid-face.'

'Oh.' Sarah ran her fingers through her hair, pulling it over her shoulder and absently brushing the long straight locks. 'Can I have it back?'

'Only if you promise not to call Henry... or text him or Facebook him. And you don't need to tell people today. Leave it for tomorrow, yeah?'

'I promise.'

Katie took the empty polystyrene containers to the bin and returned with Sarah's phone.

Sarah looked at it despondently.

'Henry's texted twice. I can't read them. Will you do it?'

Katie took the phone and read the messages.

'I can't believe you cancelled our wedding over the phone. You've got no idea how this is going to fuck things up for me.' The first one read.

Then several hours later: 'You better make sure you cancel everything. I want nothing to do with it. Tell me when it's done.'

'Nothing important, just said to let you know when you'd made the arrangements.' She deleted both messages and handed the phone back to her sister.

Sarah folded her arms, tucking the phone into her armpit.

'You need to stay here tonight? For a few nights?' Katie asked.

'Hmm? Yeah. I'll get some clothes and stuff tomorrow. I'll find a house-sitting deal or something while I look for a real place. I won't be in your hair too long.'

'You stay as long as you need to. There are already five of us here, it's not like one extra person is gonna make a difference.'

Grant will probably complain, but he can get fucked, Katie thought.

'Thanks.' Sarah lay back down on the couch and Katie left her to it.

10.

Phone tree

Sarah woke up in Katie's bed for the second time and realised she was alone. Katie often worked out before heading into the clinic. She said it got her pumped up for the day.

Sarah had a shift at the hospital starting at five p.m., and she needed to make some of the dreaded phone calls.

Her guest list was relatively small, but they were all close friends and family. Henry would have to take care of his guests. The worst call would be to her mother. It had been Hannah's dream to see her girls married off. After the divorce she'd become more and more obsessed with weddings.

When Katie came out as a lesbian there were tears. Their mum said was disappointed she couldn't have a big wedding for both of them. It didn't take her long to accept Katie's sexuality; she and Sarah had spent many evenings bemoaning Katie's poor taste in women.

While she played happy families with Henry, it had been Katie who got the matchmaking advice from Mum. Sarah dreaded having that matchmaking now directed at her.

She made her first call. 'Greta, the wedding is off.'

'You're kidding me?'

'Nope. Can you sort it out?'

'Jesus. I... I'll still need my full fee.'

'Of course.'

'I'll get in touch with all the vendors, I'll do my best to get the deposits back, but I can't guarantee anything.'

'I know you'll do what you can. Thank you.' Sarah hung up and sighed. At least that took a few things off her list.

She worked her way from acquaintances to close friends, leaving her mother for last. Each conversation was exactly the same as though they got some perverse pleasure from hearing the details. It was exhausting.

By four o'clock Sarah had spoken to everyone except her mother and she knew she didn't have time to get some stuff from Henry's place—it had ceased to be her home already—and get to work in time if she called her mother now. She'd put it off till last but now she'd run out of time. She would have to do it tomorrow.

She rushed to the apartment, changed into work clothes, shoved as much as she could into whatever bags she could find and rushed out. Henry had left his gym clothes on the bathroom floor and she caught herself picking them up.

He can clean up after himself for once, she thought, and dropped the stinking T-shirt back where she found it.

Work was busy, and Sarah was glad of the distraction. She finished at eleven and when she slipped into bed beside her sister she was exhausted, but unable to sleep. The only thing to stop her mind from going around in circles would be to call her mother, but she had to wait till morning. She stared at the ceiling and started counting her breathing; one for the inhale, two for the exhale, over and over until she fell asleep.

11.

Don't let the door hit you on the way out

Sarah got up the next morning, after being woken by Katie falling back onto her while trying to put on her shoes.

'Sorry,' Katie muttered, hopping out of the room with one shoe half on.

Sarah tried to get back to sleep but it was no use. It was time to face telling her mother.

But first she needed a coffee, breakfast and a shower. She flicked through her Facebook newsfeed on her phone while she munched on toast with peanut butter and banana. When she looked at the time it was after ten. She'd already wasted a couple of hours procrastinating.

'Hullo, darling,' Hannah answered.

'Hi Mum.'

'Are you alright? You sound funny. You're not getting a cold are you? That would be disastrous.'

'The wedding-' she broke off and coughed, she had said it so many times but this one was different. 'I called it off.'

'Sorry, love, you're breaking up. What did you say?'

She didn't believe for a moment her mother hadn't heard. 'I cancelled the wedding. It's over, I dumped Henry.'

'Why would you do something so stupid?'

'He doesn't care about me.'

'Why? What did he do?'

'Nothing, that's the point. He wasn't there. He spent his whole life at work.'

'You know men have to go out and bring home the bacon. It's what they're designed to do. It's what makes them happy.'

'Let's not have this argument again,' Sarah said. She rubber her hand across her forehead.

'I don't know what you mean. We're not arguing.'

Sarah sighed.

'You're sure you can't go through with it? It's not just cold feet? Nothing I can say to change your mind?'

'No. Things were always going to be the same and I didn't want to spend my life waiting for Henry to make time for me.'

'You know I'm not one to say anything but, you're throwing your life away. You're not getting any younger you know.'

Sarah clenched her jaw. 'I have to go. I just thought you should know.'

'Have you told your father?'

'Yes.'

'He thought this was acceptable, did he?'

Sarah started to count her breaths up to ten in her head. *Don't let her get to you.* 'He said he wanted me to be happy and there were other fish in the sea.'

'Typical. He's always managed to find someone to keep his bed warm for him.'

'Right, bye.'

'I'll come and see you, we need to talk this through,' Hannah said.

'No, we don't. I have to go. Talk to you soon.'

'Alright. Bye.'

It felt like the weight of every conversation leading up to this one sat on her shoulders all at once. It always astonished her how cruel her mother could be without even trying. Hannah had been hurt by their father's infidelity, it had eventually led to their divorce. It had gone on for their whole marriage, according to her, and by the time the girls were starting school she refused to turn a blind eye anymore.

Her parents' marriage had started with her mother thinking she could fix her father, and her father who was only interested in himself. Sarah couldn't start her own marriage the same way.

Discovering the Franklins

She was still in her pyjamas, ones she'd picked up hastily from the bed the night before. They still smelled like Henry. He liked his cologne to be pervasive, musky, almost nutty. Sarah had never particularly liked the way he smelled, she could admit it to herself now they were over.

Perhaps if she borrowed some of Katie's clothes and washed all of hers she wouldn't have to smell her ex on everything.

She wasn't rostered to work today, so she told herself to get her shit sorted out. If only she could have decided to leave three months ago. Or six months ago when he'd finally set a date, or eighteen months ago when he'd proposed and she'd known it wasn't working but she'd said yes because it's what you do. Because he'd made a scene and she was swept up in it.

I suppose it's better late than never, and at least this way it's slightly less legally cumbersome, she told herself. She walked into the bedroom and slipped into a pair of her sister's jeans. She had to roll up the hems. They wouldn't have been baggy on Katie, she had more muscle on her and her arse had always been full. A couple of times Sarah had tried to put on weight, instead of being skinny and weak, but no matter what she did she stayed the same long, thin, wispy beanpole.

By the time she managed to get to Henry's apartment it was nearly midday. She'd stopped on the

71

way for moving boxes and a few of those big striped bags; the kind everyone seems to have when they move house and at no other time. She dragged them all into the little apartment and dumped them in the middle of the lounge. Worrying about whether Henry would get shitty about the mess didn't sit high on her list of priorities.

She threw her books into a box without looking at how she packed them. It would no doubt annoy her when she went to unpack and she'd labelled every box 'misc'; she didn't want to run into Henry.

The day was mild, but Sarah quickly started sweating. She'd packed everything she owned in the lounge room into five big boxes. The sheets and towels were all Henry's. Most of the stuff in the kitchen too, anything that wasn't his he could keep.

She dumped her clothes into the striped bags. *I'm going to have to cull some of this stuff, I haven't worn this for ages*, she thought as she filled almost an entire bag with shoes. The gym clothes Henry had left on the bathroom floor were still there.

Just before six that evening, she heard the key in the door.

'Fuck,' he said. He had walked into the room and stubbed his toe against one of her boxes of books. He was wearing a middle grey suit today, with tan suede shoes. They were likely scuffed now.

'I didn't expect you home this early,' she said.

'I came home to change.' His eyes moved over the half-empty book shelves. 'You didn't waste any time.'

She wiped her hands on her jeans. 'I thought you'd appreciate it, given how much you like efficiency.'

'You're a real bitch.'

'What?'

'You're just going straight to moving out.'

'I want my stuff and I don't want to see you, so this seemed like the best solution.' She ran her sleeve over her face, the salt from her sweat stung her eyes. Henry stood there, she thought he might say something else, but he walked past her into the bedroom.

'Do whatever you like, Sarah. You always do,' he yelled back to her.

She didn't have anywhere to put all the boxes, so she taped them up and stacked them in the corner of the lounge. She'd have to ask Katie if she could store them in her shed. She could ask Hannah, she had room, but it would be more trouble than it was worth.

The four striped bags were unexpectedly heavy and awkward to carry. She could only manage one at a time. Henry stood and watched her as she took each one down to her car.

'I'll be back for the boxes. You can keep everything else.'

'As if I'd let you take it.' He folded his arms.

'Weren't you going to meet people?'

'I'm waiting till you're done. I don't want you left alone in the house.'

'For God's sake. What am I gonna do, rip up your expensive shirts?'

He looked his watch.

'This is the last one. Hopefully you won't be here when I come back for the books. I'll leave you the key when I'm done.'

'You're not getting your rent back for the rest of the month. That's mine. You've fucked everything up with your self-centred bullshit.'

'My self—' she stopped herself and took a breath. Picking up the last of the striped bags she shuffled out the door and pulled it shut behind her. She wanted to slam it, but she would have had to put the bag down to do it.

12.

Mister Winthrop

Katie believed that her job as a physio meant she needed to be in peak physical condition. She trained hard at the gym at least four times a week and played footy on the weekends with the Collingwood B team. She'd never been quite reliable enough in her accuracy to make it into the top team; her kicks went wide more often than she liked, and she had a reputation for being a body slammer.

Footy should be a rough sport. She never tackled in the back and always below the neck; she wouldn't put anyone at risk of a serious injury. Even so she'd landed awkwardly on a woman from Footscray last season and dislocated her shoulder. Katie felt guilty even though it was part of the game.

She wanted people to like her.

Her first bookings of the morning were often early; seven thirty or eight on a good day. Mostly young, fit types who'd injured themselves playing sports, but sometimes she got chronic complaints or older clients.

On Monday morning her first appointment was at eight o'clock. She jogged to the gym, did a thirty-minute intense workout then jogged to work where she showered and changed. Her uniform consisted of plain black pants and a burgundy polo shirt with the clinic's logo on it. The shirt and pants were one hundred percent polyester; she hated the way they made her sweat. She'd raised her dislike of the shirt with the clinic's owner, Joshua, a man in his mid-sixties with a marathon runner's body, but he'd said 'no reason to change them until they wear out.'

'Hey Janet,' Katie said, giving the receptionist a wave as she walked out to the clinic waiting room.

Janet was on the phone and nodded. Katie came around the desk to look at the schedule over Janet's shoulder. Her first client was new: Greg Winthrop, with a hip complaint.

Katie checked the clinic room had been set up. Greg was early, and she asked him to fill in paper work in the waiting room. She made herself a green tea while he did.

'So, Mr Winthrop…'

'Greg, please,' he said. She indicated that he follow her into the room. He was fifty-five, according to the paperwork, although he didn't look it. Shorter than her

and solidly built, he had the look of a rugby player—
close cropped salt and pepper hair, and a nose which
was flattened by repeated breaking. Katie found his
watery blue eyes off-putting.

'Greg. What seems to be the trouble?'

He took her through his basic history— rugby, as
Katie had suspected, and some boxing in his youth.
He'd had a hip flexor issue for almost a year and had
now decided to treat it.

'Right. The first thing we'll do is some range of
motion tests, to pinpoint exactly where the trouble is.
I'll give you some exercises to do at home that should
strengthen the area.'

When Greg stood and went through the test
exercises, Katie watched his face and posture carefully.
In her experience older men expressed pain with tiny
grimaces and by compensating with the 'good' side.

When he had finished she instructed him to lie on
the table. 'I'd like to have a feel of the area, is that
okay?'

'Sounds fine.'

He lay on his back and she first went over the side
without pain. The muscles were ropey and tough, but
nothing else of particular note.

'Uh, where should I put my hands?' he asked.

'On your belly, if that's comfortable, otherwise
behind your head.'

It struck Katie as a little odd he would ask this after she'd already examined his left side, but she dismissed it and moved around the bottom of the table. On the right side, there was a definite difference in the size and texture of the muscles. She suspected the issue had been developing for more than a year.

As she moved her hands around the side of his buttock he threw his arm out and grabbed her shoulder. 'Oh! That's a tender spot.'

She took his hand from her shoulder, gently but firmly. 'I'll try to be more gentle.'

Katie went back to Greg's hip. His hand hovered over his groin, as though ready to grab her again if touched a sore point.

'Hop up then, I'll show you some stretches and some exercises and then I'll write down the plan for you to follow at home.'

Greg did as she instructed, and they went through the moves. As she showed him a standing stretch he wobbled.

'Can I hold onto you while I get this down?'

'Sure,' she replied, although she would have preferred her hold onto the examination table.

She offered her forearm, but Greg went for her upper arm, his hand tucked under her arm next to her chest. She had to touch people in her job, but every now and then someone put her on edge; wanting to touch her more than strictly necessary.

'You need to improve your balance too. Although the exercises should work—' She was cut off as he started to fall forward. He put out his hand to stop himself falling and grabbed her breast painfully. They were standing side by side, and Greg had turned so he would fall against her.

He fell back against the examination table.

'Let's take a break,' Katie said.

'Right you are.'

'I'll be back in a moment.' As soon as she stepped out of the clinic room she put her hand to her breast. She was sure he had left finger shaped bruises. Rubbing it made it worse, so she took herself into the staff kitchen and drank a glass of water.

She went over what had happened in her mind. How had he managed to fall that way? Surely, he'd been stable enough holding her arm.

Unless he did it on purpose, a small voice in her mind said. She shook her head and prepared to finish the session.

Greg was sitting on the client chair in the clinic room, his face impassive. 'What now then?'

She gave him a wide berth on the way to her chair. 'I'll draw up the plan for you to take home. I think we've done enough demonstrations today.'

Katie wrote out his homework then ushered him out into the reception area as quickly as she could. Her next appointment was already sitting in the waiting room, but she went back into her room and sat down. She felt queasy.

'Hi, can you get someone else to take my next appointment? I don't feel so good.' She'd called the receptionist from her mobile.

'I'm just with someone right now and I'll come in to see you in one moment,' Janet said. Katie knew Greg would still be finishing his payment.

A couple of minutes later Janet knocked on the door and came in.

'Are you okay?'

'Not really.' Katie's breast throbbed. She explained what had happened to Janet who curled her lip in disgust.

'You should tell Josh. Sounds like a creep.'

'Do you think so? It wasn't really a big deal.'

'That's what he wants you to think so he gets away with it. And next time he comes in maybe he'll be fine or maybe he'll be worse.'

Katie ran her fingers over the short hair on the back of her head; the velvety texture soothed her. 'I don't want to sound like I'm making something out of nothing.'

'It's not nothing. Tell Joshua. I've already taken care of your next appointment. You're free till ten. Go out, get a coffee, then tell Josh.' Janet turned her head slightly to the left, and then pressed a button on the headset she wore. She walked back to her desk as she chattered into the phone.

*   *   *

After a walk and a coffee and time to think about it, Katie decided the boob grab had to have been deliberate. He couldn't have fallen like that naturally. She wanted to have another shower, but she didn't have another shirt to change into.

Joshua wasn't in until the afternoon, he generally did the after-work crowd. Katie's last appointment was at three-thirty.

'Janet told me what happened.' Joshua stood in the kitchen stirring sugar into his instant coffee. Katie always wondered how he could consume so much sugar and still be so thin. It must be all the running, she thought.

'Yeah. I think I should make an official report or something.'

'I think you should too.'

'That was easier than I thought.'

'I've made sure Janet knows to only book him in with me from now on.'

'Thanks,' she said.

13.

A Pint of Carlton

Katie jogged home, only about fifteen minutes, but it all counted. No-one else was home yet, her other housemates were office workers and Sarah's car was gone. She couldn't remember whether Sarah had a shift or not. The idea of sitting in the empty house didn't appeal. She wanted company, loud music and possibly a beer. She changed out of her gym gear and noticed her favourite pair of jeans were missing.

Typical she borrows my best jeans, she thought, moving clothes around in the messy wardrobe looking for another pair.

*   *   *

When she got there, the pub was mostly empty.

'Pint of Carlton thanks, mate.'

'You're in early, our Katie' the barman said. She was a regular, she thought his name was Tommy, but she couldn't be sure. Probably only in his late thirties, his fair English skin was red and wrinkled from too much Australian sun. His thinning strawberry blonde hair didn't make him look any younger.

'I guess.'

'Chatty Kathy in the house.' His had a broad northern English accent; Newcastle by the sound.

'Yep.'

Tommy left her to nurse her beer and she watched greyhound racing on the T.V. They played loud, trashy dance music over the speakers and the whole place had a lingering odour of old beer and stale hot chips. At least the bar wasn't sticky.

Katie had two beers over two hours and then she went to the bottle shop attached to the back of the pub for a six pack to take home. A bit much for a Monday night, but with Sarah and the wedding and fucking Greg, it was justified.

Sarah was struggling to get a large, ungainly striped bag from the back of her car when Katie walked up.

'Need a hand?' she asked.

'Yeah. Thanks.'

The bag was full of shoes. Katie had no idea how a person needed so many shoes, but it wouldn't do to say.

'Been to the apartment then?' Katie asked. Sarah looked exhausted, her eyes were shadowed and she smelled of sweat.

'I ran into Henry.'

'How is he taking it?'

'He's being an arsehole.'

'Sounds about right. You wanna put this guy in the shed?' Katie grabbed the bottom of the bag.

'Yeah, is that alright?'

'Course, you duffer.'

The shed, more like a garage, had a roller door facing into the lane behind the block, and was made of sickly orange yellow bricks. Big, but about half full of items from various housemates, including at least seven pushbikes and smelled of petrol.

Katie helped put Sarah's bags into the corner with the least spiders. 'Is that all you've got?'

'And a few boxes of books,' Sarah said.

'Fark. I thought you had more stuff.'

'I sold most of it when I moved in with Henry, and the rest we gradually replaced with his designer shit. I didn't own much in the apartment.'

They walked back to the house, and Katie picked up the six-pack she'd left on the doorstep. 'Want one?'

'Yeah'

They sat on the veranda couch.

'I'm surprised how natural it seemed at the time, getting rid of my stuff. But now it feels like I was slowly being pushed out.'

'Twenty-twenty hindsight.' Katie remembered the beers she'd had earlier; she had to be careful with her words when she drank or else she'd say something she regretted later.

'If you'd told me six months ago I'd be here now I would have slapped you.'

'No, you wouldn't.'

Sarah laughed. 'You're right. I would still have been mad. How long ago did you see it coming?'

'You know I was never a fan.'

'I thought you were jealous.'

'At first... I mean, he's so different to us. Cares about money and clothes and all that. But then when you didn't turn into a Barbie doll I started to think he must be alright. Like, he didn't make you change yourself, y'know?' Katie sipped her beer. 'Then I got jealous. Especially when I'd had so many relationships never make it past a few months.'

The breeze coming over the veranda was cool and smelled of privet and jasmine blossoms. Katie hated privet, she thought they were stupid and ugly and had no point except to exacerbate her hay fever. She rubbed her finger under her nose. 'I wanted what you had,' she said.

'I didn't even have what I had.'

Katie frowned. 'What do you mean?'

'You thought I had this loving fiancé and everything was going good, but I never saw him.'

Katie looked at her sister dangling the beer bottle between her legs, her elbows resting on her knees. She started to reach out to her but changed her mind.

'I'll say this. I was surprised you called it off but not shocked.'

'Me too.' Sarah took a swig from her beer, before leaning back and resting her head against the wall.

14.

The Glassy

2013

The Glasshouse Hotel, in Collingwood, was a painted brick building on the corner of two small streets, frequented mostly by lesbians and their various hangers on. Katie, at twenty-two, went there to get too drunk and dabble in recreational drug use.

Sarah, their mother's favourite had just moved in with her boyfriend, Henry. A complete wanktard in Katie's opinion, too much gel in his hair and four hundred dollar shoes. Sarah, their mum, even their dad, seemed to be taken in by what a slick operator he was; it gave Katie the shits. They never liked any of her girlfriends the way they liked him.

Katie still lived in Mum's house despite having finished her studies. She knew she couldn't afford anything else, but Hannah was a total drag. She said she welcomed overnight guests, but the only time Katie had tried it Hannah had grilled the poor woman and she'd sworn never to do it again.

Tonight, she planned on sleeping in someone else's bed. Not usually too hard to find an interested woman; she just had to get away without becoming entangled in a something longer by accident. Lesbians were terrible at one-night stands.

Inside the pub there were a number of small rooms and alcoves. The main bar spread through two rooms in the front, where there were a few tables and tatty wooden chairs hiding in the corners. Down the corridor from the bar were the toilets, none of which had working locks. On the right was a room with dilapidated vinyl couches of indeterminate colour. To the left were a pool table and a fireplace, which they never lit; it was probably a safety hazard in a place like this. Through the pool room was another long room used for dancing. The DJ set up at the front, and the back led out into the courtyard, where smokers stood around, gossiped and hooked up.

For a Thursday, one of the busiest nights for the Glassy, the pickings were sparse. The bar was populated by old butches nursing pints of VB. The pool room held by a bevy of skinny girls wearing tiny outfits and too much make-up. Katie's gaydar didn't even ping on them, so they were probably tourists. She kept moving through onto the empty dance floor. The DJ was playing minimalist jungle house.

'Just put on some Kylie, yeah?' Katie shouted in the DJ's ear. He gave her the finger and went back to setting up the next track.

He's gonna have to lose this shit if he wants people to dance, she thought. She wandered out the back to the courtyard, were a few hardcore smokers were braving the cold to get their nicotine fix.

Katie's nipples hardened under her tight muscle shirt, she crossed her arms across her chest to hide them.

'Oi, fuck face! Haven't seen you for ages!' A voice carried across the gloom towards her.

Katie knew the voice. 'Shaz, you shithead, how's it going?' The two women hugged and patted each other on the back roughly.

'Ah, same old, you?' Shaz offered her a cigarette, which she accepted. It would give her something to do with her hands.

Shaz sat with a group of other women who were all wearing shirts buttoned all the way up and black jackets. Katie stood in the cold while the others chatted about their domestic situations.

'We got a kitten the other day,' said the woman on Shaz's left.

Are you fucking serious? Could you be more of a cliché? Katie thought. 'I'm going in for a dance, sounds like they've changed the DJ. Thank fuck.' She walked away, and the others barely interrupted the flow of conversation to remark on her going.

The half an hour or so she'd been out the back had made all the difference; the dance floor was busier but couldn't yet be called heaving. The DJ had been replaced by a thin Asian woman spinning classic dance anthems.

Katie got a beer and stood back watching the dancers. She liked to observe from the wall looking over potentials in the crowd before making her approach. She'd also sobered up a little during her intermission in the courtyard and needed the Dutch courage to kick in.

She had her eye on a group of women, perhaps in their late twenties, who seemed to be single. She got a fresh beer then sidled to the group.

The little knot of women widened to allow her to dance with them when she approached. Everyone in the group was shorter than her, even the ones wearing heels. Katie kept to herself for a couple of songs, waiting to see if any of the group would make their move on her.

Justin Timberlake's *Sexyback* came over the speakers and she knew it was her moment. The lady closest to her had long blonde hair, a natural looking tan and short orange fingernails. She shimmied along to the song, really getting into the groove. Katie moved towards her, putting a hand on her waist. The blonde grabbed the hand, turned her back to Katie and started to rub herself against her.

When the song ended, she turned to Katie and planted a drunken kiss on her. It may have been one song, or three before they came up for air. Their kisses were sloppy and urgent.

'I'm Katie.'

'Johanna.'

'Come here often?

She laughed and flicked her hair. 'Yeah, pretty often.'

'Cool.'

Johanna kissed her again and Katie ran her hand down her front, pressing it across her pubis. Johanna pushed back against her hand.

'I'm not into toilet sex,' she said, moving Katie's hand back to her waist.

'Should we go somewhere else then?'

Johanna paused to think about this for a minute. 'Buy me a shot for the road and you can come over.'

'After you,' Katie swept her hand in the direction of the bar.

*　　*　　*

When she woke up in Johanna's bed the next morning her head was pounding. Johanna snored next to her, a cat had draped itself across her legs and she was naked.

The sex had been good, as far as she could recall. Johanna had certainly been into what she could do. She looked at her watch, just after eight.

Time to slip away and hope she doesn't wake up, Katie thought. She found her jeans, top, bra, socks and shoes easily but couldn't find her underwear. She looked around Johanna's crowded bedroom for as long as she dared.

They'll have to be a write off, she thought. There's nowhere else she could look without making a racket.

Katie pulled a scrap of paper out of her front jeans pocket and scribbled a note.

'Thanks for last night, see you around.'

No doubt they'd run into each other in future, the Melbourne gay scene was small, but she told herself she could run out as long as she left a note.

15.

My Perfect Wedding Day

2017

'I'm sorry, I couldn't get the deposit back from the caterers, which I guess is fair enough, they'd ordered quite a lot of the food for the reception already. I convinced the venue to give you half the deposit back, as well as a full refund from the florists,' Greta said. She'd woken Sarah up when she called. She felt groggy trying to understand what was happening.

'Anything that comes back should go to Henry.' It was almost noon the next Friday, the day before her wedding would have been, and she was lying on her back in Katie's bed. She'd arranged to take annual leave from then till the following Friday so she could spend some time enjoying being a new bride. There would be no honeymoon, but she'd booked the leave before that had been made clear. Now without the wedding or anything better to do she was in danger of wallowing in misery for a week.

The boxes of books which constituted the extent of her possessions were now in Katie's shed. Henry hadn't been there, and she'd left him a note with the key as she left. Pulling the front door shut she had a nagging feeling she'd left something important behind, but it would have to stay there. She determined to do her best not to speak to Henry ever again.

'Yes, I'll be able to arrange that. There is still my invoice. What's your new address?' Greta said.

Sarah flinched, she knew Henry would fight her. 'Henry is getting the refunds, so he can take your bill. He wanted all the fancy shit anyway, if it had been up to me we'd have got married in the registry office with the reception in a park.' Sarah knew her words sounded bitter.

She had to keep the moral high ground. As the one who'd ended it, she had to be exemplary in the way she spoke about Henry, at least to people outside the family.

'Right. It's a thirty-day payment, so if I don't have the money in my account I'll be chasing you for it, Sarah. I've had very little to do with Henry, and I wouldn't be surprised if he was somewhat upset about this.'

'Right. Anything else?'

'No, I think that's it.'

She waited for Greta to say something else.

'Great. Well, thanks.'

'I wish I could say it had been a pleasure to work with you, but as one of the foremost wedding planners in Melbourne, I've never been stood up like this.'

'The breakdown of our relationship is not a reflection on you.' Sarah made no effort to hide the disdain from her voice.

'Goodbye then.' Greta hung up.

'Uppity bitch,' Sarah said. She thought it seemed very unlikely Greta had never had a cancellation.

It's pretty rude to demand full payment and then insult me on top of it, she thought.

If Sarah ever planned a wedding again, she'd do it herself and it would be a much, much smaller affair.

None of this helped with what to do with herself for the next few days. Katie had offered to take her camping, but it would only be for the weekend, she hadn't booked any leave. Sarah got up and saw the bridesmaid dress, in its thin plastic dry-cleaners bag, hanging at the back of Katie's wardrobe.

Her dress was still in the boutique; she'd get no refund on that. It had been tailored to her size and shape by a woman who had said she'd won the Gown of the Year four times. It was an enormous cupcake of a dress. Henry had managed to make time to come with her to select the dress, though she suspected he wanted to make sure she had the right look for the people he'd invited.

Even if some of the guests had made plans since she told them it was off, perhaps she could get half of them together for a commiseration picnic on what would have been her wedding day. Maybe a couple of her friends she hadn't seen for a while.

*   *   *

The Edinburgh Gardens in Fitzroy were a popular place for picnics, parties, and general gatherings, especially in the warmer months. September in Melbourne could be temperamental, but the day that would have been her wedding day dawned clear; forecast to be sunny and mild, top temperature in the mid-twenties.

Sarah had created a Facebook event after her conversation with Greta. The few people who weren't online she'd called. Even on such short notice she gathered twenty of her friends to her 'Un-Wedding Day.'

The decision not to invite her mother had been hard. Dad would be there, but Hannah was still being cruel. Sarah needed people around her who would reassure her, tell her she had done the right thing and they loved her. In her gut she knew Hannah couldn't do that yet.

Discovering the Franklins

Sarah and Katie arrived together a little before midday to ensure they grabbed a good spot. Several children's birthday parties were already underway. They set up the folding table and camping chairs Katie had found in the shed.

'I dunno whose they are, but I'm sure no one will mind,' she said.

The guests arrived in clusters, each of them carrying food. By half past twelve, the nominated starting time, ten of them were sitting with blankets, chips, dips, bread, and cheese and sparkling wine flowing.

Sarah's work friend Ned had brought a small but powerful sound system which played an inoffensive classic rock playlist.

'Thanks for coming,' Sarah said as each person arrived. Everyone put on a smile and appeared cheerful; she'd asked people not to talk about the break-up.

As it approached two o'clock, Sarah spotted her mother walking across the grass towards them. She was wearing a dress that was far too short and far too red for a woman her age. Sarah thought she'd probably bought it for the wedding and wanted to wear it.

'Why is she here?' she asked Katie.

'What do you mean?'

'I didn't want her to come. I specifically didn't invite her.'

'Shit, sorry, I told her last night. I didn't mean—'

'She's going to ruin everything.' Sarah crossed her arms in front of her chest.

Hannah had come with a bottle of bourbon and a large bottle of coke. 'I thought you were probably drowning your sorrows.'

'Don't,' Sarah said.

'Don't what? Don't care about my daughter in her hour of need? After she cut off her nose to spite her face?'

'Did you come just to insult her?' Katie stood up facing her mother.

'Well, since she didn't invite me, yes.'

Hannah drew closer and Sarah could smell her. 'Are you drunk?'

'I'm fine.'

'Great. Just great.' She wanted her mother to leave but forcing her to go would cause a scene.

'I'll take those.' She took the bottles and turned to Katie. 'You keep her away from me.'

Katie nodded, draped her arm over their mother's shoulder and steered her towards the food.

'Isn't that your mum?' Ned asked.

'She wasn't invited. And she's three sheets to the wind.'

'Is she mad about the wedding being off?'

'Mad is one word for it.' Sarah tried to smile. Ned was a good friend, but she often thought he had the subtlety of a chainsaw.

'How's work?' she asked.

'The usual.'

She looked at herself, jeans and a green button up blouse. Not what she thought she'd be wearing today. She looked at the group of people who had gathered for her; they were nice enough, but she somehow felt they didn't really know her. She couldn't blame them, she didn't know herself very well. The person she'd been before she started seeing Henry, one who read prize winning books and won at scrabble, had been replaced by a woman who watched reality T.V. for fun and had let her friends drift away.

'Have I been a shit friend?' She turned to look at Ned.

He frowned, opened his mouth then closed it again. 'You've been a bit anti-social.'

'I wanted to go out with Henry, to go as a couple, but he was always too busy.'

'We invited you to things because we like you. Whether Henry came or not, didn't matter.'

'Wouldn't it have been weird if I showed up to a housewarming or something without my fiancé?'

'Only if you made it weird.' Ned put a hand on her knee. They were sitting on the grass under a big oak tree, the ground around them was sticky with sap.

'I thought people might, I dunno, pity me if I went out without him.'

'Maybe some people would have. It's funny how we expect couples to be a unit at all times. It's probably unhealthy for two people to spend all their time together.'

'It's not healthy to spend no time together either.' She sipped her sparkling wine, she was glad of the cool buzz it left in her mouth despite it having a sour aftertaste.

'I thought you'd banned talking about the break-up.' Ned smiled.

'I did...why was he such a fuck-knuckle?'

'I don't know, honey.'

'I know I called it off, but I still feel like it's his fault,' she said.

'Seems fair. It doesn't sound like he did much of a job as a boyfriend.'

'He was having an affair with his work.'

'Emotional cheating.'

'Yeah. Fuck him.'

'Fuck him.'

Sarah leaned over, and Ned wrapped his arm around her shoulders. 'You did the right thing.'

'God, I hope so.'

16.

Mother knows best

As afternoon wore into evening the party wound down. Sarah had become drunker than she expected and looked forward to going home.

Home to my sister's, she thought. She hadn't yet been able to bring herself to look for somewhere else to live.

'Katie. I love you. Thank you so much for letting me stay. I don't know what I would have done.'

'It's fine. I love you too.' Katie patted Sarah's head where it rested on her shoulder.

'But it's not fine though, is it? You've got your life. You don't want your big sister squatting in your house. Here, I'll give you some rent money.' She grabbed her handbag and started searching it for her wallet.

'It's fine. Really. Look, stop it. You're drunk.'

'I'm not drunk.' Sarah hiccupped. 'I'm a little bit drunk.'

'Here you are, my two babies,' Hannah said, hugging the girls from behind.

'Mum! I love you, Mum.' Sarah tried to awkwardly return the hug.

'Now you're back on the market, Sarah, you must let me introduce you to the son of a woman I know from work. He's a banker, so that will be nice for you.'

'I don't want to go straight back into a relationship. I mean, I don't even have a place to live, why would I want to go on a date?'

'You can come back to live with me. I have a spare room,' Hannah said.

'No!'

'Sssh,' Katie said.

'When did you turn into such a cow?' Hannah said.

'What are you on about?' Sarah replied.

'Let's not fight in front of everyone,' Katie said.

'I didn't even want you to come,' Sarah said.

'Maybe it's time for you to go home, Mum,' Katie said.

'I'm glad I've raised you to stick together, that's a virtue. It is not a virtue to use it against your mother,' Hannah said.

Don't you say it, Sarah thought.

'After everything I've done for you.'

'Fuck off. Just fuck right off. You haven't done shit for me in the last ten years. I've been trying desperately to please you and all you do is tell me I'm a disappointment.'

'I have never said that!'

'Oh please. You don't have to say the words. I understand.' Sarah stood up. 'I didn't invite you here, Hannah. I want you to leave.'

'I don't have to stand here and be spoken to in that way.' Hannah stood, her hands on her hips. Sarah knew she wanted an apology, and she wouldn't get one.

'Bye, Mum.'

Katie sat silent on the picnic rug between them. Hannah harrumphed loudly, turned and left.

'That won't be the end of it,' Katie said.

'No.' Sarah felt nauseated and headachey, she no longer wanted to be drunk. 'Give me a hand packing up?'

*   *   *

Katie drove the car, piled high with picnic leftovers, rugs, chairs and empty champagne bottles to go in the recycling. Sarah looked like she might fall asleep, her head back against the headrest, her eyes closed and her mouth drooping open.

'What happened to my life?' Sarah said.

'You'll be alright.'

'No, seriously. I had it all. I had a boyfriend, I was getting married, I had a good job and friends and he had plenty of money. Everything that's supposed to make me happy.'

'I know.'

'I was miserable. I tried so hard, you know? I tried so fucking hard.'

'I know, babe.' Katie didn't know what to say. She reached over and squeezed Sarah's knee.

They had arrived at the house and were parked in the street outside. 'You did the right thing.'

'But everything's fucked now,' Sarah said.

'It'll be okay.'

'Promise?'

'I promise,' Katie said.

Sarah opened the door of the car and vomited all over the footpath.

17.

Christmas Party

Sarah found a new place to live within three weeks. Slightly further out from the city than she would have liked, but as Henry had said, the rent she paid for their shared apartment had been less than half. She moved into a new townhouse in a block of twelve in Northcote. There were three small bedrooms upstairs. She shared the townhouse with a couple who were studying at RMIT.

Sarah had never lived in a share house before. She thought sharing over twenty-five was sad. It had taken her the whole of her week following the un-wedding party to accept she wouldn't be able to live on her own on her current salary. Not strictly true, of course, but if she lived alone she'd have to eat baked beans on toast for every meal and never go out or by new clothes.

After living with Katie and her housemates for almost three weeks she accepted it might be depressing, but not unpleasant. She had been lonely wandering around her empty flat; Henry had often left and returned in the dark. Knowing someone else was home comforted her.

Sarah had taken to making large meals the housemates were all welcome to share; she wanted to make herself feel useful. She got to know the people living with her sister and it reinforced how much she'd let her friendships slip.

In the new place her housemates were very quiet; they were out most of the day and when they were home they usually stayed in their bedrooms studying. They didn't want to share the meals she'd cooked so she had to eat the same meal for the rest of the week.

Sarah had hoped buying furniture again would be fun, but it felt like a failure. Both her parents had tried to give her second-hand stuff they had lying around.

'I don't need a handout, Dad. I'm fine, really.'

'It's not a handout, it's reducing waste. There's no reason for this stuff to be sitting in my shed when you could be using it. And I'm not going to throw away a perfectly good mattress and bed.' Graham said.

'Okay, I'll take it. It better not have springs that stab me in my sleep.'

'If it does, then you're welcome to buy a new one.' He'd smiled at her and it warmed her to know she'd made him happy.

*　　*　　*

October and November went past in a blur of routine. Henry ignored her, her mother seethed. Sarah refused to spend any time with Hannah; the blind date she'd threatened didn't eventuate; something to be thankful for at least.

Before she knew it, Christmas loomed and she had to get used to the idea she would be single at the family Christmas lunch. For the last five Christmases she and Henry had had to attend two celebrations, to negotiate which family would get the coveted Christmas day lunch, the other family left with the choice of Christmas Day dinner or Boxing Day lunch. Henry's family usually won, they had big affairs with forty or fifty people where Sarah's family's gatherings were less than ten.

'You going to the work Christmas do?' Ned asked her, straightening some paperwork one evening shift.

'Why? Are you thinking of not going?' she replied.

'No, I'll go if you're going. They're always a bit of running the gauntlet, you know, people you work with getting into the wine. Anything could happen.'

'Last year, the most exciting thing to happen was the unit manager from Intensive Care pashed the skinny dude from IT out the back. I keep myself nice.'

'Is that what you call what happened at your un-wedding?' Ned asked.

It had been months, but it still brought her to the brink of tears to think about. 'Now now, below the belt.'

'Sorry. I'm just teasing.' Ned patted her forearm. He'd gotten her through some tough shifts, and while reliable, he often said exactly the wrong thing.

'Enough of that,' she said.

Ned finished his paperwork and went home, Sarah had another four hours to work. She knew she had to allow herself to grieve, but still being so raw worried her.

Maybe I'll have a chat with one of the counsellors, she thought. She had no qualms going to the doctor for a physical pain, why should emotional pain be any different?

* * *

The hospital Christmas party was always in the first week of December. Many sections of the staff took most of December and January off. The emergency staff had to stagger their leave; the holiday period was one of their busiest times.

They had a social club; for five dollars a month they organised mixers and trivia nights. The social club people did most of the work organising the Christmas party, although it all had to be approved by Human Resources and paid for by hospital administration.

Almost four hundred staff were expected, so the venue had to be big. This year it was a warehouse in the Docklands. The tab was generous, the finger food fried, and the decorations obnoxiously red and green.

The social club organisers wore Santa hats or reindeer ears, all of paediatrics did too, they were always keen for a costume, but Sarah hated wearing them. She knew everyone was in costume, but she thought they were staring at her.

She arrived at the warehouse in a short-sleeved floral dress, mostly white with big red roses printed on it. Nice but not too nice. It came in at the waist and flared out in the skirt in a fifties style. She'd bought it on a whim with Katie who said she needed cheering up.

There were only a few people on the hospital staff she would consider hanging out with outside of work. She soon spotted Ned, standing near the bar with a bright red drink in his hand.

'I didn't realise they were putting cocktails on the tab,' Sarah said.

'I know what the quality of the wine is at these things, so I thought I'd start with a couple of strong, festive beverages, and then when I care less, I'll switch to red.'

'I'll know you've gotten stuck in when your teeth are purple.'

He stuck his tongue out at her. 'Nice dress.'

110

'You don't think it's too much?'

'Nope. Very festive.'

A huge space with very high ceilings, the warehouse still felt empty when there were hundreds of people in there. She moved around mingling with various groups and trying not to get too embroiled in workplace politics. She stuck with the white wine, chilled. She found it easier to drink than the red.

One of the doctors from oncology, Cameron, seemed to take a special interest in her. He wore a bright red bowling shirt, black trousers and shiny black shoes.

'And how's your wife?' she asked. He had a gold band on the ring finger of his left hand.

'It's not going so well, if I'm honest. I moved out a few weeks ago.'

'God, I'm so sorry,' she said.

'You weren't to know. I haven't quite brought myself to take it off.'

'You don't have to explain yourself.' She sipped her wine and wished she hadn't asked.

'Let's not talk about that. Didn't I hear you had a narrow escape recently?'

'Wow, who hasn't heard? It hurt. I still have moments where I'm convinced it was a mistake.'

'I can understand that.'

A nurse from oncology, Sarah knew her face, but couldn't bring her name to mind, came to join them and the conversation went back to work.

Cameron kept looking at her in a flirtatious way, although it could have been the wine. When the nurse looked away he wriggled his eyebrows and rolled his eyes and Sarah giggled.

'I don't see how it's funny, Sarah.'

She had no idea what had just been said. 'No, of course, sorry.' She tried to squash her smile, but Cameron kept making faces behind the nurse's back.

Eventually they were alone again, and he leaned close to her ear. 'You wanna go outside for a bit?'

'Sure. It's quite stuffy in here.'

As they walked through the open doorway onto the wharf, he grabbed her hand and tugged her towards the water.

'Hey, careful.' Sarah wobbled a little as they walked. *I might need a break from the wine,* she thought.

'I'm glad there's no one else out here.'

'Why?'

In answer he put his hand on her face and kissed her. He had short stubble, the texture a shock after years of Henry's obsessively clean-shaven skin. He smelled like musky cologne and wine and a little of sweat. A perfect combination to confuse her senses.

'Is this a good idea?' she asked.

'What? Having a bit of innocent fun at a party?'

'It's a work party, and we're both recovering.'

'So, let's comfort each other.'

The temptation of a warm, hard, masculine body pressed against hers, the loneliness she held from the breakup and before, and the wine all made it impossible to resist.

'Alright, let's get out of here,' she said.

They got in a taxi and went back to her new place. She hoped her housemates would be asleep.

*   *   *

When she let herself into the townhouse, Cameron tried to get his hands up under her skirt. He'd been handsy all the way there in the cab and Sarah just wanted to get inside the house without him grabbing at her thighs.

'Stop it. My housemates are asleep,' she said. They walked into the darkened house. She hoped they were asleep.

'Sorry,' Cameron said, his voice booming in the small house.

He wrapped his arms around her from behind, kissing her neck. She wanted to enjoy the sensations but couldn't relax standing in the living room in the dark.

'Come on,' she said. She dragged him up the stairs behind her and into her bedroom.

As soon as they were safely out of range of prying eyes, she relaxed. He put his hands on her hips and guided her backwards. Her legs came up against the bed, and she sat heavily on the side of it.

He rubbed his cock through his pants, she could see it clearly outlined against the black fabric. He started to undo his belt.

Sarah had hoped there would be a little more grace and foreplay before they got to this, the alcohol she'd had at the party had started to wear off. His cock was thick, of average length and bent slightly to the left.

He stroked it; he was clearly ready. 'Come on babe, just put it in your mouth like a good girl.'

She cringed but said nothing. She leaned forward and sucked him for a while. As she did her arousal started to return. She ran her hand up the inside of her thigh and started to rub her clit through her knickers.

'Oh yeah, touch yourself,' he said. He watched her fingers for a moment before pulling himself away from her mouth.

'Take them off and scoot up the bed.'

'Let me get a condom,' she said.

'Do we have to?'

'Yes.' She frowned, surprised she had to have this conversation with a doctor.

'Fine.' He pouted like a child but soon distracted himself stroking his cock.

She pulled off her knickers in as seductive a manner as she could manage; it didn't feel very sexy. She lay back on the bed and Cameron climbed between her legs.

Because he was thick and crooked, she gasped a little as he slid inside. It didn't take long for her to start enjoying herself. She pulled him into her and groaned.

'Mmm, you like that? You slut,' he said, panting above her.

'Uh, yes.' She didn't really like being called a slut, but it didn't seem the right time to say so.

'Oh fuck, you're gonna milk me dry, you dirty whore.'

Sarah closed her eyes and tried to focus on her body not what he was saying. Then he shuddered and grunted to orgasm.

Cameron rolled off her and flicked the condom into the corner of the room. They were both still mostly dressed. He stripped his clothes off and crawled between the covers. Unsatisfied and a little embarrassed by the whole thing, she took off her dress and hung it over the back of a chair.

It probably needs a wash now, she thought.

18.

Wake Up Cameron

Sarah woke up and remembered what she'd done. It had all seemed like a great idea last night, while she was horny and drunk. Cameron slept beside her, close up his nose dominated his face and his breath was rancid.

She'd slipped away for a shower after he'd fallen asleep. When she lay next to him, clean, a creeping sense of shame washed over her. Nothing wrong with a one-night stand, nor a rebound shag, but with this man someone she had to work with, it felt like a mistake. She'd listened to his enormous nose whistling and snorting all night and hadn't slept much.

The light of the morning slanted into her bedroom through the blinds and she wondered how long she would have to tolerate him before she could get him to leave. It looked like he had no trouble sleeping in a strange bed, something she often struggled with, nor sleeping beside a strange woman.

She compared him to Henry; taller, broader and fatter. And older, only by a couple of years, but she added it to the list of reasons to regret sleeping with him.

She got out of the bed, slipped on her sea-green satin dressing gown and headed downstairs. Still cool in the early morning air, she knew it would build to a scorching day. In the small courtyard she watered her pot-plants and squinted against the powerful early sunlight.

When she went back inside, her housemate Leon had made a plunger of coffee.

'You want one?' he asked.

'You're a lifesaver.'

He smiled as he pushed the black plastic knob down. Sarah watched the tiny waves of the coffee as the liquid squished up through the mesh and the grounds were forced to the bottom.

'Did I hear someone else come home with you?' He passed her the coffee. The smell combined with the lingering scent of the sunlight on her robe invigorated her a little.

'Sorry, did I wake you?' Her mind returned to the animalistic grunting Cameron had made. He had been vigorous but finished a long time before she would have. Then he rolled over and fell asleep.

'No, studying. I just wondered.'

'A guy from work.' She looked at the floor and shook her head.

'Ah. No good, then?'

'A lady would never comment on such things,' she said.

'But you don't deny it.'

'He's still upstairs.'

'Oh.' Leon took a sip from his coffee.

If she'd liked Cameron more, she would have made a fresh plunger of coffee and taken it up to him. She used to do it for Henry on the rare occasions she woke up before he left.

She took her cup and sat on the step leading into the back courtyard. At this time of the morning the steps were in shade, and she could look out over the swaying ferns. A trail of ants wavered their way across from the clothes line to the fence. Above her the sky so bright she couldn't look at it for long.

She put the cup down and closed her eyes. She had to go and face Cameron. Waiting till he woke could be hours. She finished her coffee and put the cup on the sink.

Upstairs she could hear Cameron snoring from the top step. She opened the door and started to dress, making as much noise as she could. He was still fast asleep when she finished.

She prodded his shoulder; no response. She poked him harder, and he moved a little but didn't wake.

'Cameron. It's time to get up.' She gripped his shoulder tightly and shook him.

'Get off.'

'Come on. You have to get up.'

'Leave me, Nicole.'

'It's not Nicole. I'm Sarah, and I want you to go home.' It must have been his soon-to-be-ex-wife's name, perhaps not as separated as he claimed. His eyes opened, and he seemed dazed.

'Ah, shit,' he said.

'Yes.'

'Where am I?'

'Northcote. Shall I call you a taxi?'

'No, I'll get an Uber. It'll be cheaper.' He sat up and immediately lay back down. 'Get me a glass of water.'

'Please?'

He groaned. 'Please.'

Sarah went downstairs to fill a clear glass from the tap. She took a deep breath as she ascended; he was a real arsehole especially in the morning.

'Here.'

He sat up slowly and took the glass from her without saying anything. He drank it all and continued to sit there, his genitals only partially hidden by the sheet. Sarah turned her back and started to gather up his clothes. They'd come off in a hurry and were scattered around her small bedroom.

'Get dressed.' She handed him the pile.

'What's the rush?'

'I have things to do. Can you get dressed please?'

She'd made a decision while drunk she now regretted and the shame of it burned inside her. Maybe in a few days it would have calmed down, but she wanted him gone so badly she had to restrain herself from forcing his clothes onto him.

She picked up her phone, shoved it in the back pocket of her jeans and went back down to the kitchen. He obviously has no intention of making this any easier, she thought. She started to sweep the timber floors of the kitchen for something to do with her hands. Leon came past again, he had headphones on.

Leon and his girlfriend Juliette, her other housemate, were international students from South America. They were both studying for their Masters in International Studies, which seemed to be world politics from what Sarah could understand. They had the two smaller rooms in the house, they slept in one, and used the other to study. Most of the time they didn't use the lounge room at all. After living with Katie's housemates who were constantly wandering around, cooking, or watching trashy T.V. together, Sarah thought the hippy types were much better at creating a sense of community.

It had been nearly a half an hour since she went up to wake Cameron. She went back up the stairs, stomping heavily this time, she flung her bedroom door open and saw he'd fallen asleep again.

'Cameron. Get up.'

He groaned.

'Get up. This isn't your house, you have to leave.' She shook him by both of his shoulders. His hands came up and batted her away, but she wouldn't stop. She kept shaking him until his eyes snapped open and he stared at her with unveiled hatred.

'Let me sleep.'

'Go home and sleep,' she said.

'I can't go home to Nicole smelling like some cheap tart.'

'I don't know why I thought the line about you being separated would be true. Never in the history of doctors and nurses has it been true.'

'Can I at least have a shower?'

'If you promise to do it right now and then go.'

'Fine. I got what I came for.'

Sarah found a clean towel and threw it at him. She pointed to the bathroom and went back downstairs. She was hungry, and her hangover started to sink its claws into her brain. She heard the shower come on and she filled a glass of water from the tap knowing it would make the water run hot.

Cameron came down the stairs, his dark hair looking oiled with dampness. 'I'll wait for the Uber outside. See you at work.'

'Yeah, see you.' She closed the door behind him and her legs turned to jelly. She made it to the couch before collapsing. The room spun, and her head had started to pound. She waited until it let up a little then went back to her bed, which now smelled like idiot doctor.

19.

Dinner with Dad

Katie and her dad liked to talk about sports and television shows they liked. Graham never asked whether Katie was dating anyone, she thought he probably wasn't ready to talk about it if she said yes.

He had never called her a dyke, and he'd always shown polite interest when she talked about a girlfriend. But he'd shift in his chair or suddenly remember he'd left the stove on. She suspected it would have been better for him if her sexuality remained unmentioned.

Sarah had quizzed him about it once and the resulting strained silence could have powered a family home for a week if there had been some way to harness it.

The two sisters were at Graham's house, more of a granny flat, in Eltham, one evening in early December. They tried to see both of their parents at least once a month, usually together so neither of them would have to answer questions for the other.

Graham's granny flat took up a corner of the garden in the back of a large, split level family home. He had known the owners since university. When he had dropped out to pursue working for himself, they'd remained friends when many of his contemporaries had let the relationship slide. He'd asked if he could stay in their flat about two years after he separated from their mother. The woman's elderly mother just moved into a nursing home and they were keen to have the flat occupied.

It had been nearly twenty years now since the split and Graham still lived in the bungalow. Katie had stopped wondering why when she left school. The marriage had ended in infidelity and he had never tried to commit to someone again.

He'd had a number of girlfriends in that time, some had been relatively serious and longstanding, but none had ever required him to move out.

'Do you think he's still seeing what's her name?' Katie asked as she drove up the long driveway.

'Um, Robyn wasn't it?' Sarah said.

'Yeah. She seemed nice.'

'They all seem nice, not very useful though.'

'That's not true. Remember the one when you were in year twelve? A sculptor who welded great whacking hunks of steel and pipes together to make garden ornaments?'

'She was cool. Probably got sick of Dad having no ambition to speak of.'

The bungalow sat among eucalypts and ferns; wild because Graham only tended them in the most basic way. Katie always felt like she'd stepped into a rainforest when she visited. He had a few delicate-looking orchids hanging in baskets, their bright pink and yellow flowers adding colour to the sea of green and brown.

It would be light for another couple of hours, but the overcast sky gave everything a silver tint like an old photograph.

'Heard you on the drive,' Dad said, standing in the door as they approached and stretching out his arms to embrace the two of them together. Katie couldn't remember the last time he'd hugged them one at a time. It had started as childhood fun and had continued ever since.

'Hi Dad,' the two sisters said together.

'I hope you brought your appetites. Lovely big trout I caught the other day in my mate's dam. I'm roasting it in salt and lemon, it should be almost ready.'

They followed Graham in, the lounge, kitchen and dining room were all one space, with a bedroom and en suite bathroom at the back. He had a circular pine table with four pine chairs around it. The chairs were covered in grey fabric with a texture like small pimples. It reminded Katie of carpet. There was one couch which folded out into a bed for guests, and an armchair, both covered in shiny floral material fraying on the armrests. The kitchen, more accurately termed a kitchenette, had a stovetop, oven, sink, and about thirty centimetres of green laminate bench space. He'd cut a piece of board which sat perfectly over the sink for added bench space when he chopped vegies.

It smelled of roasting fish and citrus; Katie's mouth watered. The table, laid with plastic place mats, knives and forks with blue plastic handles, held a large green salad and a potato salad both big enough to feed twenty people.

'You've gone a bit overboard there, Dad.' Sarah said as she sat at the dining table.

'I make sure my girls have plenty to eat, and besides, anything you don't finish I'll have for leftovers. No downside.' He grinned.

'You must have been an Italian *Nonna* in a past life '

'I wish I could cook well, but alas...'

They all sat at the table and Graham served them sections of the steaming trout to go with their salads.

'Have you spoken to Henry then?' he asked. Since the un-wedding party, the sisters had been to see their father twice and he hadn't mentioned it.

Sarah spluttered. 'Uh, recently?'

'You know, since you jilted him.'

'I didn't leave him at the altar.'

'You did leave it quite late,' he said.

Katie scooped herself some more potato salad. 'No good going through with it. He'd shown he wasn't giving the relationship what it needed to thrive. So, Sarah left it a bit late, at least she realised before we were all standing in the winery and the celebrant asked if there were any objections.'

'Would have been a very expensive way to say I don't. And you had no idea earlier?' Graham asked.

'I kept hoping he would get better, he would step up and give me what I wanted. I guess I don't really understand why his job demands so much of him all the time. I think he liked it, it made him feel important to be indispensable,' Sarah said.

Katie thought about it for a moment. 'If he'd really wanted to spend time with you, he could have made time.'

'I hoped he'd realise I was an important project too, but he didn't.' Sarah had started to cry quietly. She wiped her eyes and went to the bathroom.

'She's still pretty sensitive about it, isn't she?' said Graham.

'Does that surprise you? It's only been a couple of months. You were a mess for years after the divorce. You thought we didn't notice, but we did.'

Graham poked the trout on his plate. Katie had meant to be cutting but perhaps she'd gone too far. Dad might look tough, with his work-hardened hands and wild greying hair, but he had never quite learned to manage his feelings.

When Sarah came back in Katie gave him a stern look she intended to convey they weren't to talk about the wedding.

'How's work?' he asked.

They stayed on the safer topic of Sarah's work for a while before Graham turned to Katie and asked the same question. The first thing that popped into her mind was Greg Winthrop's not-at-all-accidental fall. She rubbed her forearm across her chest remembering the pain.

'It's going alright, you know, same as always.' She didn't want to tell him about Greg. She hadn't told anyone except Janet and Joshua. There should be no shame, it hadn't been her fault, and yet she didn't want people to look at her with pity. She'd once told Sarah about some kids at school who were harassing her because she was gay. She hadn't come out at school, not officially; she'd tried to convince herself she'd grow out of it, but the other students taunted her anyway.

Katie would never forget the look on Sarah's face: anger, fear, hatred, pity, powerlessness. A combination of emotions she never wanted to see again, and she worried if she told Sarah about Greg, she'd give her the same look.

'I gave a client to Joshua a while ago because he was a real pain in the arse, he's apparently decided not to come back, so read into that what you will.' She regretted saying it immediately.

'What makes someone a pain in the arse?' Graham asked. Sarah said nothing, perhaps waiting for additional information.

'Oh, you know, he had a bit of a wandering eye. Nothing serious.'

'Why do I think there's more to this?' Sarah's brows were drawn together.

'There isn't.' Heat rose in her cheeks and she looked down at the table. She hoped Sarah would take the hint and leave it.

Dinner with Graham always ended with a game of Scrabble; a tradition they'd started relatively recently, after Sarah had moved in with Henry. Sarah and Katie had made an unspoken agreement they would not play as seriously as they would have liked to, walloping their father every time didn't make it much fun.

*   *   *

'There was something with that guy at work though, right?' Sarah asked as she drove the two of them home after they finally called it a night at eleven.

129

'I don't wanna talk about it.'

'You have to tell me now, it sounds juicy.'

'Can we not? He's just a creep. I didn't want him around, so Joshua offered to take him.'

'I don't believe you, but I'll let it go for now.' Sarah's eyes were on the road, but Katie got the sensation she was being examined nonetheless.

20.

The Gardener

Something more had happened with Katie's client, but from past experience Sarah would need to wait until Katie was ready to talk. The dinner with Dad had reminded her even though she had moved house and got into a new routine, she still carried a lot of anger and pain. All it took to set her spiralling into a blubbering mess, was the mention of Henry's name.

At least he hasn't tried to set me up with anyone, she thought. It didn't seem very likely, her father tried to be involved but he had drifted away from them when they were teenagers.

She had invited him to the un-wedding party, but he hadn't turned up. Instead her mother had arrived, uninvited. She still hadn't forgiven Hannah for that. She had never asked why he hadn't come, he said he would do his best, which given he would have been at her wedding in the Yarra Valley otherwise, seemed odd.

After her reaction to his questions earlier, she didn't want to go over it with him, but she was hurt.

Ned had stopped asking her how she felt. When she'd found her new place he had offered to help her move, but she'd said no. She only had enough stuff for two car loads. Maybe he thought she'd rejected him, but she couldn't understand why someone would want to help her move house if he didn't need to.

To make it up to him, she invited Ned out to coffee on the following Tuesday. They met in a narrow café squeezed between a yoga studio and a bar in Brunswick.

As they were sitting on the uncomfortable plywood bench seats— she assumed they were supposed to look rustic— Sarah's mind kept coming back to the question: 'What are you doing with your life?' She felt like she'd shut herself down to the basics; work, eat, sleep, repeat.

'…and Mum wants me to bring trifle for Christmas—'

'I need a hobby. Or a group, or something to do in my time when I'm not at work,' she said, cutting him off.

Ned looked stunned for a moment but recovered quickly. 'Uh, okay. What do you like?'

'I don't know. I like reading.'

'You could join a book club.'

'It doesn't sound very exciting,' she said.

'What about something a bit more active? Outdoors?'

'Yeah?'

'Let's go see what CERES has. They might have some working bees or activism stuff you can join,' he suggested.

The café was about five minutes' walk from CERES, a community space which took up a couple of acres and housed to a number of vaguely-connected areas and projects. At the front a large adobe style building which housed a café and a room for educational programs for school children. Behind that and down a hill, a model house, demonstrating how architecture could be harnessed to create economical living spaces. Further back an old train held craft workshops, another café, and a bicycle repair collective which had amassed an array of bike wheels, inner tubes, tyres, and other miscellaneous parts all stacked against the wall of the shed.

Between the education section and the bike shed, were community garden plots. Sunflowers reached towards the sky, their heads bobbing in the breeze, along with tomato plants and some sort of vine Sarah thought might be pumpkin.

Ned came here often; he knew the regular characters and was an excellent gardener. He didn't have a plot of his own, but he sometimes tended other peoples' plots in return for excess produce. They strolled past a man wielding a pick-axe; a shovel lay on the ground next to him, on the way down the hill towards the community noticeboards.

'Hey Nick!' Ned called. The man put down his tool and turned towards them. In his early thirties, Sarah guessed; he had broad shoulders, and naturally dark-olive skin. He wore a battered straw hat and overalls with no shirt. Sarah caught herself staring at his upper arms and the smooth, well defined muscles.

'Hey!' He waved at them, and when he smiled his face came alive. The look of a hick farmer only extended to his clothes; he was clean-shaven, and his teeth were white and straight. He wiped his forearm over his face to wipe away the sweat. Although it wasn't especially hot, it looked like he had been working hard. As they got closer, she could see his eyes were dark brown, almost black, and he could easily have been a model if his nose had been slightly less prominent. Sarah scalded herself for evaluating him so calculatingly; an almost perfect Adonis.

'What's the haps?' Ned said.

Sarah cringed.

'Clearing out this patch for my aunt Vicky. She had potatoes in here but they went mouldy and she decided she didn't have the strength to pull them all out herself.

I've seen her lift vats of tomato sauce the size of a small cow, but this she can't do.' He smiled again, and Sarah forced herself not to stare.

'Was she maybe giving you something to do? Are you working these days?'

'Here and there. Nothing official, just odd jobs. It suits me when I want to buzz off to a festival or something but sometimes you hit a dry patch and you end up doing stuff for relatives. Are you going to introduce me?'

Ned looked at the ground for a moment, his face colouring slightly. 'Yeah, sorry. This is Sarah. We know each other from work. Sarah, this is Nick. We went to high school together. He's a great dirty hippy now, while I have a real job.'

'Real jobs are overrated,' Sarah said.

Nick wiped his hand on his overall before holding it out to her. 'Very pleased to meet you. I'm not normally quite this scruffy, but you can't get stuck in unless you're willing to get dirty.'

'Sounds about right.' She smiled. She found herself struggling to think of anything to say. Luckily the two men had plenty to catch up on, so she stood back and listened to their banter.

Sarah tried not to stare at Nick, but the sun on his golden skin, the daggy hat, casually leaning on the pickaxe, all made her want to watch him. Work-roughened, dark, quick to laugh and so different to Henry.

'We were trying to find Sarah a new hobby. She wants to expand her horizons,' Ned said. Sarah snapped back to focus on the conversation at the sound of her name.

'Oh? What do you like to do?' Nick asked.

'I like reading, but that's not very social or energetic. I thought I could try something outside. Something to meet people and get out of the house. Know of anything?' Sarah asked.

'How do you feel about community clean-up stuff? There's lots of work needs doing regularly down Merri Creek to keep the litter and weeds down.'

'That's a great idea,' Ned said.

'Not what I had in mind, but it does tick all the boxes. I could give it a try and see how I like it.'

'Sure. It's mostly organised on Facebook, so maybe we can add each other as friends and I'll make sure you get the invites and info.' Nick smiled his dazzling smile again, and she almost believed he'd come up with the suggestion as a way to keep in contact with her. She shook her head slightly.

Don't get cocky, he isn't interested in you, he's just being nice, she thought.

As she and Ned walked further on, towards the train carriage and the noticeboard on its side, she felt herself grinning.

'I didn't pick you as a litter picker-upper,' Ned said.

Sarah looked at the noticeboard for a while before she answered. 'No. I didn't either.'

'Nick has that effect on people; he can make you give up your time for just about anything. He's currently on a clean waterways bent, before that it was dumpster diving and food wastage, and before that he worked with kids in poverty in Argentina.'

'Sounds like he really follows through on his passion.'

'Yeah. He tends to charity-hop. Whatever is the issue *de jour*, he'll follow for a year, two at the outside, before he gets onto another bandwagon.'

'A year or two volunteering is a pretty good run, isn't it?'

'Sure. I dunno, I think he gets bored.'

Bored is not a virtue, she thought, even if, by some stretch of the imagination, he was interested in me, then he might be bored of me just as easily. On the other hand, maybe a year or two with him is worth it. I don't need to go into every relationship thinking it's for the rest of my life.

21.

The Royal Oak

Katie played footy on Sundays. She'd been playing with the same team for four years, but she couldn't kick a reliable goal. She practised and practised in her first couple of seasons. The coach had given her extra time after the games, but nothing could get her consistent. Sometimes she'd punt one and it would sail through the goal posts dead-centre; other times she'd kick from the same spot, same wind, same everything and she'd miss completely.

She'd never make it into the A-grade team. They needed players who could kick on target.

Perhaps if she could get her head around the physics, the coach, Abby, tried to explain to her then she'd be able to understand what made a kick work. It always made sense as Abby talked, but as soon as she stopped, and Katie tried to put it into practice it might as well have been brain surgery.

Training each week started with an hour or so of drills; running forward, backward, sideways, skipping, then tackling, handballing, kicking, and other general skills. Towards the end they'd play out a few strategies and finishing with warm down and stretching. After four years of twice a week training, games on the weekends, gym four times a week and jogging to and from work, Katie was fit.

Her housemates and her friends all told her she exercised too much. Katie thought they were just jealous.

This is what it takes to be an athlete, Katie told herself. She trained when she had a cold, or was tired, or didn't want to. Going to footy training when she was emotional was always the worst.

In the weeks following Sarah's sudden cancellation of the wedding, Katie had struggled to keep herself together. She knew Sarah needed her; she had to be the strong one this time. For what felt like the first time in their lives, Katie felt no jealousy towards her sister.

When someone was sleeping in her bed, she'd been tempted more than once to skip her exercise and catch up on the sleep she missed. Sarah had tossed and turned; probably bad dreams.

Now she had her room back, Katie was lonely. She'd always been content to be alone, she'd had girlfriends, but none of them had lasted longer than a couple of months.

With Sarah there, she'd had a taste of coming home to someone, to hear them breathing, sometimes snoring, in the night. She hadn't understood the comfort it brought until she'd experienced it. Of course, it was only her sister, but it made the lack of a partner feel so real it hurt to breathe.

There were always people hanging around the ground when the team trained. They were partners, or friends of the team, dropping off or waiting to go to the pub later. In the couple of months since Sarah had moved out, there was one face Katie kept seeing on the side lines.

As it moved into summer the nights became lighter and milder. There were more people hanging around watching them train. Katie remembered faces, especially when they were as gorgeous as this one.

Her hair was dark brown, shaved all the way up the left side and artfully messy all down the other. When the wind caught the long side and whipped it across the woman's face, she left it dancing in front of her black eyes. Her smooth skin was the colour of a well poured café latte, tattoos peeked out of the top of her shirt, and from the ends of the sleeves.

One particularly hot November night, Katie had watched her rolling up the cuffs of her shirt, distracted by the slow revelation of the black tattoos. As her attention wandered from the game the ball slammed into her face.

She'd tried to be more a part of the game after that but knowing the woman with the creamy skin and snaking black ink was there, just out of sight, made it hard.

'You coming to the pub after?' Jessie said. She was a defender marking her during the practice game.

'Where are you going?'

'Dunno, we thought we might try the Royal Oak. It's this grotty old man pub but has fifteen-dollar steaks.'

'Sounds like a laugh. I'll come along.'

The mention of grotty old men made Katie wonder whether having a group of women football players descend on it would seem out of the ordinary. Individually they would probably have been unremarkable, but when they went anywhere as a group it felt as though they were carrying a neon sign reading 'LESBIANS APPROACHING'.

At least there would be enough of them that any drama they might get into could be avoided without being drawn into a fight.

'Cardo is bringing her friend, the dark one who's been hanging around lately. We all reckon she's got her eye on someone.'

'The one with the tatts?'

'Noticed her, did you?' Jessie wriggled her eyebrows suggestively, before rushing off towards the ball which had been kicked in their direction.

The rest of the practice went by without Katie taking much notice. The mysterious friend stood down at the other end of the ground and she had to strain to see her. Tight black jeans and a plain black shirt hugged her body.

The girls showered quickly and met out the front of the pavilion. It was getting towards nine but none of them liked to eat before training; Katie always felt sick if she tried to train hard on a full stomach.

'This is Nell. I said she could come to the pub with us.' Cardo, a short, stocky woman who played in the midfield, introduced the woman with the tattoos.

'Hi Nell,' they said in unison.

'Hi.' Nell put her hand up in a sort of half wave. *Doesn't talk much*, Katie thought.

*　　*　　*

The pub was too bright inside; lit by fluorescent bulbs hanging on chains from the ceiling. The bar was covered in bogan memorabilia, AFL players from the eighties, and signs with slogans like 'Beer 'n' Bullshit Area'. Two counters ran through the middle, at the far end of the room horse races filled the screens, one screen showed rows of text and numbers. Katie assumed they were odds or stats, something she had no interest in.

Just as Jessie had promised the fifteen-dollar steak special came with a pot of beer. Katie had VB, then everyone ordered the steak.

They found a table in a corner. Carpet the colour of pool tables and furniture of dark wood made the room feel weathered. The whole place seemed to have stepped out of time, even the old fellas sitting at the bar were slightly faded, like old photographs of themselves.

'What do you do for work, Nell?' Katie asked. She immediately scolded herself for asking the most obvious question.

'I work in a library.'

'Bullshit,' Jessie said.

'For real. In the city.'

'I didn't think librarians looked like you,' Katie said. She'd hoped it would be funny but when it came out it sounded sleazy. She looked down into her beer and waited for the heat in her cheeks to go down.

'And what about you, Katie?' Nell said.

Katie looked up. 'Sorry, miles away. I'm a physio.'

'Yeah? That's cool.'

Katie looked up and Nell smiled at her. Nell's appearance seemed to have been carefully cultivated to be distancing; the tattoos and shaved head. It said 'I do not want to talk to you.' On the other hand, when she smiled Katie thought there might be a chance for something more.

'Yeah, it's alright.' Katie grinned. Nell's intense eyes flicked back to Cardo and they moved on to gossiping about the love lives of the others in the team. Cardo did most of the talking; her particular skill was to know everything happening with the team.

Their food arrived, Katie got another round of VB to drink with the steaks. With a full belly and a couple of beers under her belt she began to relax. She caught herself staring at Nell several times.

It's just coz she's sitting opposite, where else am I gonna look, she told herself, but she didn't entirely believe it.

'Geez, it's late,' Jessie said looking at her watch. 'Nearly eleven.'

Katie had to be up early. She wasn't looking forward to it. 'I'd better head off too.'

'Lovely to meet you, Katie,' said Nell.

As they were leaving Nell stood very close to Katie, waiting until the other two headed for the door before she spoke again.

'I've had my eye on you. Give me a call sometime.' She slipped a piece of folded paper into the back pocket of Katie's jeans. The feeling of Nell's hand across her buttocks made her clench involuntarily.

Nell walked purposefully towards the door before Katie could think of anything to say. She followed, not quite sure if her feet were still attached to the bottom of her legs.

22.

Boyfriend Material

When Sarah got home from her coffee with Ned she sat down and looked for Nick on Facebook, but she worried it would seem too keen if she friended him the same day. His profile didn't have much she could access, but he had a few dazzling photos. She took her time staring at each one, telling herself he would never know so it wasn't creepy.

The next day she worked a very early shift that ended up being extended by three hours when one of the other nurses called in sick. Her legs ached, and she could easily have gone straight to bed when she got home at seven. She heated up some leftover lasagne she kept in the freezer for the times she didn't have the energy to cook, then she sat in front of the T.V. and finally sent the friend request to Nick.

*   *   *

Ned was already there when she arrived for her shift the next day.

'I see you're friends with Nick now.'

'Yeah,' she said.

'I got the feeling you were checking him out the other day.'

'I...yeah, a bit.'

'I have no problems with you being interested, but I feel like I should tell you a few things.'

'Oh?' She didn't like where this was headed. Could Ned be jealous? He had become oddly protective of her since her split from Henry.

'I mean he's fun and hot, but he's not boyfriend material.'

'Why do you say that?'

'I know a few people who've come out of... liaisons with him pretty messed up. He can be - I suppose thoughtless is the word.'

Henry had been thoughtless, and unavailable. Should she be considering a relationship with someone with the same flaws as her ex? On the one hand she had plenty of experience dealing with it, on the other she'd probably end up in the same place.

'Thanks for the heads-up, but I'm not really ready to date anyone. Just looking.'

Ned raised his eyebrows in a way that probably meant he didn't believe her. He could believe what he liked, she knew she had no intentions of dating Nick, even if he looked like a Greek god.

During her shift, she couldn't have her phone with her, so she couldn't scroll through his profile. But whenever she had a spare moment, her mind drifted back to Nick; wondering what he was doing, and what sort of bad boyfriend he would be.

Thoughtless could mean a lot of things. He might forget to go on dates, or not make time for his girlfriends among his many causes. But it could also mean being dismissive or even cruel, albeit unintentionally. A thoughtless man could forget you were sensitive about the size of your breasts and make comments on them.

She didn't think she could deal with someone who didn't remember what she liked. Even Henry, for all his time at work, knew her. He never asked her to change, he remembered she didn't like coriander, and would ask to have it taken out in restaurants without prompting. He even kept track of what her parents and sister liked; quite an achievement, given the amount of time he would have spent with them over the life of the relationship.

He did care for me, in his way, Sarah thought. With all the time at work she never questioned if he was with another woman, it seemed so out of character. Their sex life had been pretty tame, and usually she initiated. At one point she asked him outright if he liked sex.

'To be honest, I don't think about it much,' he'd said with a shrug. Just a low libido then, but it still added to her loneliness. In her next relationship she would ask for more. She'd make sure they spent quality time together and had a hell of a lot more sex.

'What exactly did you mean by thoughtless?' she asked Ned.

'You know, jumps from cause to cause and runs off to festivals and stuff. He'd just do things without thinking about the relationship. One girl he dated had arranged to take time off her job to go with him to a protest at a big mining site in Queensland and by the time it came around he'd lost interest. He'd made arrangements to go to a festival in the bush up near Beaumont instead. He hadn't even told her. She went to Queensland on her own and when she got back, she dumped him.'

'What a dick. Why are you still friends with him if he treats people so badly?'

'He's fun. He knows where the great parties are, and he is tapped into some excellent recreational narcotics.'

Sarah was silent, Ned painted a pretty poor picture of his friend.

'I've known him since high school. It's hard to stop all contact with someone you've known so long. He just sort of shows up for a while and then I don't hear from him for a year.'

At the end of her shift, Sarah checked her phone and had a Facebook message from Nick.

'Hey! Cool to meet you. If you're keen to get started we're doing a creek clean-up this Sunday from 8 a.m. We'll probably wrap up by about 11, don't wanna be out in the heat of the day. Let me know. I wanna get to know you better ;).'

It all seemed straight forward except for the winking emoji at the end. It could be he used it a lot and it didn't mean anything, but it could easily be flirting.

'Cool. I'll be there,' she replied. She could afford to have a carefree fling with a hot dude. He might not be boyfriend material, but he could be her rebound guy.

23.

Merri Creek

Sarah tried to remember the last time she'd woken up early on a Sunday when she didn't have to work. Even with all the wedding planning and Henry's early morning gym sessions, she'd managed to sleep in on the weekends.

She hadn't slept well the night before. The idea of spending the morning with Nick had made her heart race, her mind swirled with scenarios of how she might turn the meeting into sex. In the end she'd watched some porn and masturbated before sleep came over her.

Her morning routine usually included toast with avocado and coffee, but she didn't want coffee this early. She felt tired and jittery; caffeine probably wouldn't help with that.

The Merri Creek runs for about seventy kilometres through the northern suburbs of Melbourne until it joins the Yarra River in Abbotsford. A popular walking and cycling trail runs beside it from Coburg until it joins the

Yarra trail. The clean-up crew were working an area next to the St Georges Rd bridge in Fitzroy North.

Sarah had been over the bridge hundreds of times in her life, but she'd never been down to the creek there. The wide concrete path had long grass on either side and despite it being a warm day already, she wore long pants and hiking boots to protect her in case there were snakes.

Nick was already there, laying out dirty white canvas bags and rubbish picker tools on a patch of short grass beside the track. He wore scruffy dark green pants and a faded black T-shirt. The shirt pulled tight across his muscular chest.

'You found us!' Nick said as she came down the hill from the road.

'Your directions were spot on.'

'Thanks.'

He explained the basics of the rubbish collection, and next week they would be back to pull some of the non-native plants out. There were three others working; an older couple and another woman. They looked like they were old hands at this, and Nick stayed with Sarah.

'You know Ned from work?' he asked after about half an hour.

'He and I do the same sort of work. When we're on the same shifts it's much more fun.'

'He's been telling you stories about me, hasn't he?'

'No... not really.'

'You don't have to coddle me. He's got it in for me for some reason. He never comes out and says it, but I suspect he got a bunch of nonsense from my ex.'

'He hasn't told me much.'

Nick looked up from under his battered straw hat. Her cheeks coloured under his gaze, she knew she couldn't lie well. 'He did tell me one story.'

'The Queensland trip?'

'Yes.'

Nick shook his head. 'I knew he took her side in that whole thing.' He looked down at the ground and stabbed an old chip packed with his rubbish picker. Sarah waited; he would tell her his version in his own time.

'The thing is, we both knew the relationship was on the way out when that trip came up. She doesn't like to tell people we'd talked about ending it. I wanted to go to the protest, but I knew going with her, trying to take care of her, she'd never been to something like that before, all of it would just really ruin my vibe.'

Sarah stopped picking up rubbish and stood watching Nick. His head bowed, looking into the grass.

'I told her she should go to Queensland on her own. We'd finish up when she got back, I'd move all my crap out of her place and whatever. She didn't want me to stay in her house while she was away, which is fair enough I guess. It would have been a painful reminder to her, so I arranged to go to a festival while she went north.'

'Oh,' Sarah said.

'I don't know why she tells people I did it behind her back. Maybe she needs to make me the bad guy. I understand her being hurt it didn't work out. But I'm disappointed in Ned. I've known him half my life, to believe her instead of me.'

'Ned can be complicated.' Sarah wanted to believe Nick, he seemed genuinely saddened by the story, and his words sounded true, but why would Ned have sided with the ex over his friend? He wasn't someone who changed his opinion easily; he would defend his friends. She wanted to believe both of them. Perhaps the truth lay somewhere in the middle.

As she watched Nick's forearms, the lean muscles moving as he picked up pieces of rubbish, she knew she would have a very hard time saying no if he wanted her.

24.

Call me

Katie wasn't used to being pursued; she had always been the pursuer. She spent three days getting up the nerve to call Nell.

The first couple of days she told herself she couldn't call because it was too soon, but she knew she really wasn't ready yet. Her confidence with women had not recovered from the last break-up. That relationship had lasted six months, the longest of any of her relationships.

Eliza was a broad-shouldered, stout woman who knew what she wanted. She did freelance journalism work on LGBTIQ issues for various charities when they wanted to get an issue out into the public consciousness. She had a lot of contacts: members of parliament, heads of organisations, and even some corporate high flyers who could get some money directed to projects if they were pitched right.

Eliza seemed much more interested in the idea of being in a relationship than in Katie. She needed to be seen to be gay in the community.

'When are you going to move in with me?' Eliza had asked abruptly one evening.

'What? We haven't talked about that.'

'Isn't it the obvious next step? People know you, the networks are keen to have you as part of events. It would make us official.'

'I like living on my own and having my place near work.'

'Don't be stupid, your place is a trash heap. You can't be taken seriously living like that.'

'Living like what?' Katie asked.

'Didn't you ever wonder why I don't visit you? Why I always have you over at my place?'

'I never thought about it.'

It didn't matter what she said. If she wanted to stay with Eliza, they would be doing things her way, or not at all.

'So, when are you going to move in?'

'Couldn't we think about getting a place together? I mean, your place is so far out of the city. What's in Belgrave you want to stay for? I wouldn't be able to jog to work. I'd have to get up at five to cycle to work and that's without factoring the gym in.'

'For God's sake, just get another job closer to my place.'

'You expect me to give up my house and my job? And it'd be too hard to train with the footy team. That's everything in my life. You want me to give it all up?'

'You don't love me enough to make a few sacrifices?'

Katie scoffed. 'It's not a few sacrifices, it's everything. And I don't like the fact you just expect me to agree. No compromise, no discussion.'

They were silent for a moment. Katie thought maybe she was reconsidering.

'I guess if you don't want to live with me, then there isn't much point in being in a relationship is there?'

Eliza always ended every argument by saying she didn't love her enough and they may as well break up.

'I never said I don't want to be in a relationship with you.'

'Well, that settles it then. You'll move in with me.'

'Haven't you heard anything I've said?' Katie always gave in to Eliza but that day she decided she wouldn't.

'You said you wanted to be in a relationship, so I assumed you had agreed to move in.'

'Yes, you assumed. I don't want to live in Belgrave. I'm not willing to give up everything I love for you.'

'So now what?'

157

'I'm quite happy to discuss moving in with you if you're willing to move too.'

'You know that's not an option. Everything I love is in the hills,' Eliza said.

'That's exactly what you just asked me to do.'

'You've got a football team and a job you could do anywhere. It's not the same.'

'It is the same. You never think about how things affect me.'

'If you think I'm that bad then why are we even together?' Eliza folded her arms across her broad chest and frowned like a sullen teenager.

'You're right. We may as well break up,' Katie said.

Eliza stayed silent for so long she wondered if she'd run out of things to say.

'No one has every broken up with me,' Eliza said finally.

What choice did you leave me? Katie thought. 'I'm sorry.'

'You're not fucking sorry. You'll never be in a long-term relationship if you don't learn to compromise, Katie.'

'You're right.'

I'll know not to give away so much of myself next time, she thought.

*   *   *

Katie had this running through her mind every time she'd picked up the phone to call Nell. She knew it hadn't been all her fault the last relationship ended; Eliza had been manipulative and controlling. The doubts in herself had started early and Eliza had fed those doubts with every disagreement.

It had surprised Katie she'd given up on the relationship so suddenly, but it had all become clear. Once she'd seen the way Eliza manipulated her, she couldn't stand it.

On Sunday she came home from the game and decided to call. She put the phone to her ear and listened to the ringing for a long time.

'Shit. You there?' Nell seemed out of breath.

'Yes, hi! It's Katie.' She'd been sure it would go through to voicemail. She didn't know what to say.

'Hi!'

'So, you said to call.'

'Yes. I like you. I think we should go out.'

'I like you too.'

'On a date, in case I wasn't clear.'

'Yes, I got that.' Katie had no idea what to say to Nell; she didn't to do small talk.

'When are you free?'

They arranged to meet on Tuesday, when she had no footy training. The whole phone call lasted five minutes and thirty-seven seconds and had been mainly awkward silences.

I guess some people aren't good at phone calls, Katie thought, and she smiled to herself.

25.

White Wine Talking

After finishing the clean-up along the Merri Creek, Nick offered to take them all out for coffee. Sarah declined, she decided she needed to sort out who, if anyone, had told the true story about Nick's break-up. Even if he wasn't going to be her Mr. Right, she didn't want to be hurt.

She had plenty of time to mull over the different versions of the story before her next shift with Ned on Friday.

'How did the creek clean up go?' he asked.

'Yeah, good.'

'Was it?' His upper lip curled as if he was disgusted.

'There's no reason to look at me like that. You introduced us, if he's such a bad guy you should have cut the conversation off before I got sucked into volunteering with him.'

'I didn't expect you to fall for him right there.'

'I haven't fallen for him,' Sarah said.

'Like hell you haven't.'

She couldn't deny she had a strong attraction to Nick; he was beautiful and mildly exotic. From another world, free spirited and wild. But Ned had his reservations and she trusted Ned with her life.

'Even if I have, I'm not looking for a relationship right now.'

'I've heard that before.'

'Not from me you haven't!'

'No,' Ned sighed. 'Not from you, but from others who said they wouldn't fall for Nick and did anyway. I should have known you were rebounding. This is all my fault.'

'I can make decisions for myself.' Sarah put her hands on her hips. The more Ned told her to stay away, the more she wanted Nick.

'I know, just be careful, okay? I don't want your heart broken.'

'I don't want that either.' She smiled. *Just like Ned to try to protect me from things in the most backward and roundabout way.* If what he said was true, then she would do well to stay away from Nick. If only the image of his skin shining in the sun would get out of her head.

*   *   *

When she got home from work her housemates were upstairs. The classical music they put on to study wafted down. She looked around the lounge room, with its slightly tatty second-hand couch bought online, and the table and chairs she'd taken from Katie's shed, and remembered what her life used to be like.

This time three months ago she'd had a beautiful black leather lounge suite, a full bookcase and entertainment unit which took up most of wall facing the couch, a glass-topped dining table with six black leather chairs. Her bed had been handcrafted oak with an orthopaedic mattress. Nice things that made coming home feel welcoming but there had never been anyone to come home to. Now she had people to come home to, but she knew almost nothing about them and her furniture reminded Sarah that her life was far from settled.

She didn't think she needed things to make her happy, but without the things she'd had with Henry, she didn't know who she was anymore. Some people might have been excited to start again, but it felt like hard work. She had to find the person she'd been before she gave up most of her interests and personality to do what she thought Henry wanted her to do.

My Friday night is watching TV at home on my own, great, she thought. She flicked it on, poured herself a glass of white wine and sat down. She hadn't heard from Nick since the weekend. She knew she shouldn't, but she sent him a text message.

'Hi.' She didn't expect him to reply. He'd be out at some warehouse party or secret show.

'Hey. What's happening?' he replied within a minute. 'At home. You?'

'I'm at a party but it's crap. Wanna go for a drink?' 'I'm not really up to leaving the house,' she wrote. 'Shall I come to you?'

She hesitated, if he came over, they would laugh and drink wine and she would almost certainly end up sleeping with him. The last time she'd had a man in her bed after a few wines he'd turned into a complete fuckwit as soon as daylight came. Would Nick be different? Ned said he couldn't be trusted, but she could use the company.

'I'm almost out of wine, if you bring some we can drink it at mine.' She sent him her address.

'I'll be there in 20min.'

She looked down at herself; sweaty and still wearing her uniform after a shift. *I'll just have enough time to spruce myself up before he gets here.* She showered, brushed her hair, and put on a clean pair of jeans and a pale blue patterned T-shirt. He buzzed the doorbell as she came down the stairs.

'You found it okay?' she said.

'Yeah. Nice neighbourhood.' He stepped forward and pulled her into a tight embrace. She could smell him, patchouli and beer and his skin smelled like he'd been in the sun.

'The party was no good?' She took the wine he offered, a rosé, and waved to him to take a seat.

'Full of posers. I couldn't have another conversation about veganism with someone drinking bourbon and Coke. Those big companies are fucking up the world faster than the farmers.'

I just wanted some company, Sarah thought, and now he's going to lecture me. 'I didn't know that,' she said.

'Sorry, I can't stand hypocrites. I get a bit ranty when I've had a couple. You have to tell me to shut up.' He smiled, she felt warm as though he was the sun god he resembled.

'It's okay. Don't get me started on doctors who smoke.'

He laughed, and she handed him a glass of wine.

*　　　*　　　*

They sat and talked until Sarah started to yawn.

'I'm keeping you awake,' he said.

'I had a long shift at work. Sorry, I'm okay.'

He looked at his watch, a chunky, battered, leather-banded thing. 'It's after midnight, perfectly respectable to be tired.'

'Are you?'

'Not really.'

A beat of silence sat between them, she looked at his lips, they were full and he'd grown some dark stubble since she'd last seen him. It made him look older, and somehow more real. She leaned towards him, he smelled so good.

'I don't think that's a good idea.' He put his hand on her shoulder.

'What?'

'We've had a whole bottle of wine since I got here, and I'd had a few before that. I suspect you did too.'

'Oh.' Sarah felt like she might burst into tears.

'It's not that I don't want to, I mean it's why I offered to come over, but, maybe I'll just sleep on the couch for now.'

He may have been right, but she still felt rejected. She stood up and had to sit down again. 'I think I might be drunk.'

'Do you need a hand up the stairs?'

'I should be alright. I'll just go slowly.' She stood up again and this time she was prepared for the wave of dizziness. She steadied herself by grabbing the back of the couch and trailing her hand along the wall to the stairs.

'See you in the morning,' he said, flicking off his shoes and settling into the couch.

*　　　*　　　*

Discovering the Franklins

Sarah woke up early the next morning, she hadn't closed her blinds and the light had moved to hit her straight in the eyes. Her head hurt a little, not too bad. She threw a dressing gown on over her nakedness and went downstairs.

Nick slept, sprawled on the couch which wasn't quite long enough for him. She smiled, glad he'd stayed. She tiptoed past him, her feet on the floorboards almost silent, got a glass of water, and started heading back up to bed.

'Good morning,' he said softly.

'I thought you were sleeping.'

'Not quite.' He sat up and patted the cushion next to him.

'Water?' She offered him her glass.

'Thanks.' He took a long drink. In the early morning light, with his hair sticking out everywhere from sleep, he looked delicious. He put the glass on the coffee table and she moved closer to him, her thigh pressed along his. She looked into his eyes, their blackness sharp despite the hour.

He returned her gaze steadily and leaned towards her. Their lips met, and it was all the sweeter for being sober. He kissed her gently, his lips explored hers.

'Do you want this?' he whispered.

'Yes, yes.' She didn't care where it went. He was there, touching her, awakening her. He pulled her into his lap and wrapped his arms around her without breaking the kiss.

She heard a soft thud upstairs, took his hand and led him upstairs to her bedroom.

She pushed the door to her bedroom closed and leaned her head against it.

'Wouldn't want my housemates to catch us,' she said, slightly breathless.

'How very conservative of you, Sarah.' Nick smiled a Cheshire cat grin and moved towards her. She felt the heat of his body as he pressed against her. He wore a workman's singlet and khaki shorts; it had been hot the last few days. He'd been wearing a short-sleeved button-up shirt last night, she wondered where it had ended up.

He moved his face close to hers and took a deep breath. A flush of arousal and embarrassment crept up over her chest to her cheeks.

'You smell fucking great,' he mumbled into her neck. His lips grazed her skin, nibbling at her. She remembered she was standing, panting against her bedroom door, and her knees trembled.

Ducking out from under Nick's arms, she moved to the bed. He followed her, she could hear his breathing as he approached, an animal waiting to ravish her; she liked the idea.

'What do you want, Sarah?' he said. He stood at the foot of the bed, looking up at her, she rested her weight on her elbows and examined him. He lifted up the hem of his singlet revealing a hint of tight, golden brown abs. 'Is it this?'

'Mmm,' she mumbled.

'I can't hear you. What do you want?'

'Take off your top,' she said louder.

Nick grabbed the nape of the singlet and dragged it over his head, his muscles rippling. She wore only a dressing gown, she ran her hand up her inner thigh, parting the satiny green fabric. She stopped just below the groin.

'Now the shorts,' she said.

Nick popped open the button and slid the shorts over his slim hips. He wore no underwear and his cock stood out proudly, his arousal clear.

'Open your robe, I want to look at you,' he said.

She hesitated briefly, worried her lack of curves would turn him off.

'I showed you mine.' A grin flashed across his face; cheeky, hungry.

Sarah reached for the belt of her dressing gown and pulled at it slowly, she wanted as much time as possible to take in his glorious nakedness. Once the tie came undone, she lay her head back on the bed, her eyes toward the ceiling, and pulled the robe open across her small breasts.

She looked up at Nick, hearing him growl low in his throat as she revealed herself.

He took a step forward and grabbed her ankles. He went down onto his knees and started to kiss the tops of her feet. She giggled softly, the ticklishness of the spot and the electricity from his touch were too much for her to hold it in.

As his mouth travelled up the inside of one leg, then stopped to cover the other leg, she felt herself opening. Hot and slippery, ready for him.

He reached the middle of her thigh and she sighed and pushed her legs apart to allow him access. His eyes flicked up towards hers.

'What do you want me to do to you, Sarah?'

'I… don't know,' she said.

'Maybe I should stop then?'

She smiled. 'No! Don't stop.' She had never had to ask for what she wanted before, both confronting and invigorating. 'I want you to lick me until I can't stand t anymore.'

He put his hands on her thighs and moved them a little further apart. 'Oh yes. And then what?'

If you don't touch me soon I'm going to burst, she thought. 'Perhaps then you might like to... uh, fuck me?'

'Since you asked so nicely.' He grinned and kept his eyes on hers as he lowered his mouth to her pussy.

He created sensations beyond anything she'd ever experienced; slight flicks of the tongue, barely there, long firm, strokes and then he pressed his whole face into her, sucking and rocking against her.

'Oh God,' she cried. She grabbed his curly black hair and pushed him into her. He moaned against her, creating a delicious vibration.

Just when she thought she would orgasm, something she'd never done before from oral sex, he pulled away.

'What would you like me to do?' he asked. His eyes and his cock both said he wanted her.

She put her hand out and stroked his cock. It twitched at her touch and he let out a sigh.

'Do you think you might like to fuck me now?' She continued to stroke him, a little more firmly.

'Yes, I think that would very nice.'

She rolled over, rummaged briefly in the bedside table, and found a condom. As soon as he'd rolled in on, she grabbed his hips and pulled him down over her.

He pushed himself gently inside her; he was big and the slight resistance felt so good.

He started to thrust slowly; rocking gently. She wrapped her legs around him, pulling him closer. The exquisite delay of this slow dance between them and wanting the animalistic ravishing his smile had promised her tore at her.

'More,' she said.

'How much more?'

'Everything. I want to know how much you can give me.'

He made another growling sound in his throat, a low rumble which came up from his chest. For a moment she thought he would just tease her, but little by little his thrusts became harder, deeper, faster.

She could sense his climax building; his breathing became ragged, and he seemed lost in her body. She abandoned herself to the sensations in her body and as the wave of his orgasm crashed through him, his body rippling and spasming, she felt herself fall over the edge.

Nick lay down, partially covering her, as they allowed their breathing to return to normal. Sarah hadn't realised how inattentive and lazy Cameron had been until she lay there with Nick. And Henry, who would only ever fuck her if she begged him or when he'd been drinking. It seemed she'd missed out on a lot.

She hadn't closed the blinds, and the shaft of sun had moved. She lay back and closed her eyes.

*   *   *

When she woke again her bladder demanded her attention. She slipped out of the bed, trying not to wake

Nick, but his head came up as she opened the door. She smiled at him and he lay back down.

Now she'd taken him to bed, she didn't know what she wanted from him. To date him? Or just use him for fun? He was her most competent lover, and those lips… she started to get aroused thinking about it.

She had to be fair though; he didn't know she was an emotional mess and would probably draw him into something that couldn't last.

Nick sat up on one elbow and looked at her as she came back in. She didn't want to look at his face, he seemed so innocent and happy.

'What's wrong?'

'Nothing…I don't think this is a good idea.'

'You didn't think so earlier.' He smiled wickedly.

'I mean, I'm not looking for a relationship. I shouldn't have invited you over.'

'It didn't feel like a mistake to me.'

She looked at him, his eyebrows drawn together in confusion. 'I can't be with anyone right now.'

'I never asked you to marry me, Sarah. We're just seeing how things go.'

'I think you should probably go.' She pulled her dressing gown closer to her body and looked at the floor.

'I don't understand, but I'll go.' He put on his clothes and went downstairs.

He doesn't know how crazy I am right now, she thought.

He went to the door. She stood in her robe watching him from the stairs.

'I hope you'll feel differently later, I really like you, I enjoy spending time with you, and the sex...' He exhaled and shook his head. 'Please think about it. When you're ready, let me know.'

26.

Winthrop Strikes Back

Tuesday seemed to come quickly for Katie. She was so nervous about the date with Nell she almost went to work with odd shoes on.

After she said goodbye to her first client of the day and went into the reception area to see the next, Janet looked up at her, with a frown.

Katie stopped short and looked around. 'What?' she said, her voice low.

'That guy, Greg Winthrop. He's in with Joshua. You better hide in the kitchen.' Janet made a shooing motion at her, but too late. Winthrop had emerged from the consultation room behind her. Joshua followed him out.

'I thought you said Katie went on leave?' Winthrop said.

'Uh, she's back.' Joshua put his hand on Winthrop's shoulder, as though to shepherd him forward.

'So why can't I see her for my appointments?'

Katie frowned. Joshua had told her he'd explained to Winthrop why he couldn't see her after his behaviour.

Janet had told her he wouldn't be back in the clinic. Yet here he stood, playing dumb about it.

'I'm sure it was explained to you, Mister Winthrop.' Katie's voice stuck thick in her throat, constricted with cold anger.

'They told me you were on annual leave. I want all my appointments to be with her from now on.' He addressed the last comment to Joshua.

'That won't be possible,' Katie said.

'Why not?'

'I won't take you as a client.'

'What nonsense is this?' Winthrop asked, looking at Joshua.

Joshua's opened and closed his mouth like a stunned fish.

'If you recall, the last time you had an appointment with me, you assaulted me.'

'I did nothing of the sort. I fell trying to do the exercises you showed me. It was an accident. Could've happened to anyone.'

'Regardless, I will not see you as a client.' Katie folded her arms.

'This is outrageous. I won't stand for it.' Winthrop had puffed himself up and still addressed Joshua. 'Are you going to let her speak to me like that?'

'If you'll just settle your account, Greg, then we can make you another appointment for a fortnight,' Joshua said.

Katie glared at Joshua. How could he leave her out on her own? And let Winthrop walk all over him.

'You'll have him back to see you, then?' she said to Joshua, keeping her voice low.

'Not now.'

'It's your clinic, you can decide who comes here.'

'I said, not now.'

Katie heart beat loudly in her ears and her legs were wobbly. Greg stood at reception, between her and the staff lunch room. She had another appointment, but she was far too worked up.

'I'm taking five minutes,' she said to Joshua. He sighed, then nodded.

Katie left the clinic and walked onto the street outside. The sun warmed her shoulders and the sudden brightness made her sneeze. Drivers on their way to work passed in a steady stream. She turned left towards a small, quiet park; she fancied sitting under a tree.

Joshua didn't usually avoid conflict. She'd seen him be firm with clients who had refused to pay or had been rude to the other physios. Given how supportive he'd been when she brought the initial incident to his attention, she was surprised he'd been such a chicken with Winthrop.

I suppose the waiting room isn't the ideal place for a confrontation, she thought. She sat down on a bench, closed her eyes and took ten deep breaths in the cool, dappled shade under the oak tree.

*   *   *

When Katie returned to the clinic Janet looked so relieved she might burst into tears.

'I'm so sorry Katie. I didn't think to warn you and then he was there and... I'm so sorry.'

'Where's Josh?' Katie asked.

'He took your client.'

'Right. I need to talk to him. Are there any spots this morning we're both free?'

Janet found a spot at eleven thirty and she blocked it out.

The next few clients were hard; her thoughts kept spiralling around Winthrop and Joshua. The image of her boss, standing by as the man who had assaulted her tried to shame her into taking him back.

At eleven thirty she went into the staff room. She made herself a cup of tea and looked through the biscuit canisters for the chocolate ripples she liked when Joshua came in.

'Janet said you wanted to speak to me.'

'Yes. I think you know what it's about.'

'No. Why don't you tell me?'

'For God's sake. He assaulted me, and you let him come back. He insults me, insults you, treats everyone like shit, and you do nothing.'

'What do you expect me to do?' Joshua leaned against the table and folded his arms across his chest.

'Tell him he needs to find a new clinic. His behaviour is unacceptable.'

'He told me it was an accident.'

'Of course he did. You weren't there, it's my word against his, and he's counting on the fact you'll side with him to avoid conflict, so he can get away with sexually harassing me again.'

'I did say he couldn't see you.'

'Yes, but you lied about why. How long did you think that would last? I couldn't have been on leave permanently.'

'I don't understand why you're so upset.'

'Clearly. You didn't back me up in there' she said.

'I don't actually have proof he did anything wrong.'

'There never is. Creeps like him learn to only do it when they are alone with a woman, where she has something to lose from reporting it. When you explained why I wouldn't see him did he say women take things too seriously? Did he say I'm too sensitive?'

'Well...' Joshua hesitated.

'You didn't actually confront him.'

'No. I didn't. And I won't. I'll take him off your list to keep you happy, but I won't turn him away without a good reason.'

'Assaulting me isn't a good reason? I thought you were on my side,' she muttered. She felt sick and let down. She felt worse now Joshua didn't believe her than she did the day it happened. She couldn't bear to look at him.

The chocolate ripple biscuit she had been hunting for no longer appealed, nor did her cup of tea. 'I don't feel very well. I'm going home.'

'Come on, don't be like that. What more do you expect me to do?'

'I want to you call Greg Winthrop and tell him he's no longer welcome at this clinic because you have reason to believe he harassed one of your staff and it will not be tolerated.'

Joshua uncrossed his arms and looked down at his hands where they rested on his thighs. 'I meant, apart from that.'

'Start looking for a new physio.' Katie tossed her tea down the sink and it splashed up and over the stainless steel and tile splashback. She plonked her teacup on top of the slosh of milky tea and walked out of the kitchen.

She collected her things and asked Janet to get rid of her appointments for the rest of the day. She jogged home in her uniform, along streets which were now starting to fill with workers going to lunch.

The jog didn't take long, and Katie's stomach was still burning with anger when she got home. She changed into her running gear and kept going, on until she came to the creek. She'd been running hard and she sat next to the water getting her breath back.

I loved my job, I liked the people, at least I thought I did, what a fucking mess, she thought.

*   *   *

When Katie finally got home she was starving. There were some leftovers in the fridge and she ate them without really tasting anything. Exhausted and still a little shaky; it had been a long time since she'd been this angry.

She showered, and as the water ran over her head and face, she remembered she had a date with Nell that evening.

'I can't come out tonight, I'm sorry,' she said when she called Nell.

'Why not?'

'I had a bad day at work, and I won't be good company.'

'No excuse. You'll have a fab time with me. Best cure for a bad day.'

'I know, I just... I'd really rather do it another time.'

'Weak.'

181

Katie didn't know what to say. She hated to be seen as weak. She'd stood up to her boss, and the man who had abused her and it had only made things worse. 'Don't call me weak.'

'Scaredy-cat.'

'I'm not, I just can't come out today, okay?'

'You let me know when you're feeling less weak and I'll see if I'm free.' Nell hung up.

I don't know why I'm surprised, my taste in women has always been off, Katie thought.

*　　　*　　　*

The next night at footy training, Cardo and Jessie were both making faces at her, wriggling their eyebrows and making pouty lips all through the training.

'So, how did the date go?' Cardo said, as they were packing up.

'It didn't,' Katie said.

'What do you mean? Nell told me you were all set to go?'

'We were. Then I had a really rough day at work and when I called her to reschedule she hung up on me.'

'Did you explain what happened?' Jessie asked.

'I tried to. She's really shit on the phone.'

'I should have warned you about that,' Cardo said, chuckling.

'It really didn't help the feeling shit aspect. If she's like that at the first slight wobble, then what's she going to be like if there's a real issue down the track?'

'She's not like anything, you just caught her off guard. And she hates phone calls.'

'Then why did she tell me to call her?'

'I don't think she meant literally,' Cardo said.

'It's not the point. I don't think she likes me.'

'She likes you all right. Just give her a chance.'

'I'm not going to chase someone who cracks the shits anytime something doesn't go to plan.'

'That's not very fair,' Jessie said.

'I don't think it's very fair. She laughed at me for needing a night off after the day I had yesterday.'

'I'll get her to give you a ring.' Cardo offered.

'Don't. Just, leave it okay?' Katie zipped up her bag and walked out of the pavilion.

Jessie followed her out. 'What happened yesterday? Do you wanna talk about it?'

'It's just work stuff.' Katie was surprised Jessie had trailed after her. They weren't particularly close.

'Even so...'

'Alright. I don't see why I should keep it to myself.' Katie explained the whole story as they walked around the outside of the oval.

'No wonder you didn't feel like a date,' Jessie said.

'Yep.'

'And did he say anything about it today at work?'

'No, he wasn't in today. Conveniently.'

'Oh.'

The pause stretched out. 'What does that mean?' Katie asked.

'He might have taken your resignation seriously. Maybe you should look for another job.'

'I feel like I'm being punished for being attacked by a creepy predator.'

'It feels like that sometimes. But you can't work for someone who doesn't have your back when something like this, or worse, happens in the future.' Jessie clapped her hand on Katie's shoulder. 'It feels hard now but it will be for the best. This Joshua guy sounds like a real piece of work. Pretending to be all caring and whatever but actually not doing anything to help.'

'Maybe you're right.'

'Of course I am. Have you thought about reporting it to the police?'

'That's a bit extreme isn't it?'

'He did assault you. You'd be well within your rights to charge him. You've got a snowball's chance you'll get it to stick but it might be worth it.'

'I'll think about it.' Katie shifted her bag on her shoulder and walked home.

27.

Ethel

As soon as Nick left her apartment Sarah regretted letting him go. He was undeniably hot, great company, good to talk to and he knew how to touch her in ways she'd never known before. But she didn't trust him. She didn't trust herself either. Cameron should have been proof her taste in men was terrible right now.

'I know that look. I tried to warn you,' Ned said when she arrived at work a couple of days later.

'Yes. I didn't listen. I got seduced by the idea of him.'

'You need a hobby that doesn't involve being around men who are bad for you. Maybe a book club. They're mostly women, so you should be safe.'

'Come on, I'm not that bad.'

'I don't know what you're usually like, but lately...'

'It's two bad decisions,' she said.

Ned held up his hands in surrender. 'You're right, two is not a lot. But I worry about you.'

185

'I know. I worry about me.' She pushed her hands into her pockets.

'You gotta get to know yourself, get comfortable with being single again. A routine, an identity, outside of Henry or Nick or any other man who turns your head.'

'Easy for you to say. My mother thinks I'm a total failure, even when I was with Henry, she wanted me to be more like him and less like me. My father is basically a dropkick. My sister, well, I love her and everything, but I feel like I've spent a lot of time with her recently.'

'Where do I fit in there?'

'I didn't mean to imply you weren't important.'

It's not all about you Ned, she thought. His life hadn't self-destructed. He had plenty of friends and seemed happy to be single. It seemed so easy for him.

'I better get going, can't miss handover,' she said. She didn't look back as she walked away, but her gut told her Ned stared at her back with a hurt look on his face. She didn't have anything left in her to care about how hurt he felt when he'd been so judgemental about Nick.

*   *   *

Her day crawled past, she only had four patients to look after, and all but one of them in recovery from elective surgery.

Discovering the Franklins

The last patient, an elderly woman, had a chest infection that didn't seem to be clearing up. She was diabetic with a compromised immune system. At eighty-eight she'd had a good run, but Sarah didn't like to see people suffering. She'd hated her palliative care rounds at uni for the same reason.

'How are you feeling, Ethel?' Sarah always used the patients' names when she addressed them. She thought it made them feel important and it helped her to remember. Most of the time people were in and out of the ward in only a few days. Occasionally they would get someone with more of a chronic condition, but with the lack of funding they were always trying to get people out.

'I can't complain. My hips ache from lying down too long, my lungs feel like they're full of water, and I have an itch on my shoulder I just can't seem to get at. Would you?'

Sarah went over to her and gently helped her forward off the bed, she scratched around trying to find the right spot.

'Up a bit, no, too far. Left. Yes, there it is. Thank you.' Ethel smiled.

'You're welcome. I wish all my patients were as courteous as you.'

'They don't teach manners these days. I know there are some out there who would help me up the steps if I

187

needed it but most of the time they just watch,' Ethel said.

'That's terrible. Do you have someone to keep an eye on you?'

'My neighbour, Roger, he comes around every so often, and the neighbour on the other side, Kym, she waters the garden for me. It gets too much for me in the heat you see.'

'You don't have any children to visit you?'

'No, dear, I never managed to have any. My husband, he died some years ago now, wanted them but we never fell pregnant.' Her eyes were moist. Katie felt stupid for having brought up a clearly painful memory.

'I'm sorry to hear. I'm sure you would have made a great mother.'

'Yes, I helped a few children in my way, I fostered some when it became the fashion, but they don't have time for an old bird like me.'

Sarah fluffed her pillows and made sure she had the remote control within reach before she went back to the nurse's station to do some paperwork. The conversation with Ethel had made her feel quite emotional.

What if she never found someone? What if she never had the opportunity to be a mother? She'd always been on the pill, in one form or another, and she had no idea whether or not she could get pregnant. Henry had had no time for those conversations.

Discovering the Franklins

Sarah's shift finished at eleven so she would be there when they next drained Ethel's lungs. Although Ethel put on a brave face, she suffered a lot each time they had to do it. Afterwards she could breathe better, but Sarah dreaded the process.

As they were applying suction to the chest tube, she thought the gurgling sounded like a death rattle. She held Ethel's hand in her gloved one and squeezed it gently. The old lady was a fighter, but she doubted she'd leave the hospital this time.

Everyone had to die at some point. Sarah found it hard to watch, whether they were young or old. At least she could make sure Ethel didn't go out alone.

'I'll be back tomorrow, do you want me to call anyone for you? One of the neighbours might like to come see you.'

'I'll see them soon enough.'

'Even so, they might like the company.'

'I don't think so, dear.'

I'll ask again in the morning, Sarah thought as she pulled the curtain around Ethel and switched off the overhead lights.

*   *   *

By the time she came back the next afternoon, Ethel had died. Her bed had been cleared and someone else was in it.

'I thought she'd last longer than that,' she said to Ned, whose shift had just finished.

'Sometimes I think they just decide it's time.'

She looked down at her feet.

'Sorry,' Ned said.

'What for?'

'Yesterday. I was a jackass.'

'Me too.' She looked up at him, he wore a sad smile.

'Friends?' He stepped forward and hugged her.

'Yep.' She rested her head on his shoulder and they stayed there for a while. She didn't want to break the embrace, but she had work to do.

Ethel's death hit her harder than she thought it would.

28.

A café with a man's name

The more Katie thought about what had happened with Winthrop the angrier she became. He'd targeted her. And her boss, who had said all the right things at the time, didn't back her where it counted.

She couldn't continue to work there. Her respect for Joshua was completely gone.

'You're leaving aren't you,' Janet asked on Friday afternoon.

'I'm…I can't stay.'

'I get it. I thought about leaving myself, but I'm too stuck in my ways.'

'I should wait until I have another job to go to, but I don't know if I can.'

'I'll keep my eyes peeled for you if it helps.'

'Thanks. It's good to know someone's on my side.'

Janet looked like she might say something, but the phone rang, and she put on her telephone voice to answer it. Katie went through into the staff room for some water.

Joshua came into the room, she turned and as soon as he saw her he froze.

'For God's sake,' Katie said.

'I don't understand what's happened between us. You're being very hostile.'

'I'm being hostile? Because keeping a client around who assaults your staff couldn't possibly be considered hostile.'

'We've had this talk. You know my position.'

'Yes. I do.' She took her glass of water and walked past him out of the room.

Her employment contract stated she had to give four weeks' notice if she left. In the current climate she didn't know if she could stand to be in the same building as Joshua for a week, let alone almost a month.

She pulled out her phone with the intention of looking for jobs and saw Nell had sent a message.

'When are we going to reschedule this date? I like you, but I won't wait forever.'

How romantic, Katie thought. No, don't take it out on Nell because you're mad at Joshua.

'Weekend is pretty clear except for a game on Sunday.'

'What time is the game?'

'Kick off at 2.'

'Brunch Saturday?' Nell was clearly no chattier via text than on the phone.

'Okay.' Katie wasn't really in the mood for chat either.

Training was good, and the potential with Nell cheered her a little, although she already had doubts about their suitability.

Stop it, you haven't even had one date, don't talk yourself out of something that hasn't happened yet.

Katie managed to get through the rest of the day without resigning. She saw Joshua walking through reception a few times, but she made sure she didn't have to speak to him. She promised herself she'd look for new jobs over the weekend.

*   *   *

Nell picked a brunch place in High Street, near the Westgarth Cinema, called Garry. Katie had looked up the menu online and it seemed swanky, a little bit pricey, but good for a date.

She woke up early, showered, fiddled with her hair for about twenty minutes before heading over. The café was on the corner of a small street about a ten-minute walk from her house. The front and side were glass doors which had been rolled away, so the entire place opened into the air. It had been stiflingly hot for several days, but typical of Melbourne, today was overcast and cold.

Katie looked over the patrons who were already sitting in the café; she saw a few who had decided the weather forecast couldn't be trusted and were wearing shorts or sleeveless tops. There were always those who chose fashion over practicality. Katie had never understood it, she would always much rather be comfortable than fashionable.

'You're early.' Nell's voice came from behind her.

'So are you.' Katie turned towards the voice, smiling. She put her hands out intending to hug Nell but when she didn't reciprocate the gesture she dropped her hands again.

The wait staff said there would be a ten-minute wait for a seat, Katie saw all the tables were occupied. 'Perhaps we should have booked.'

'I don't believe in booking for brunch. That's taking it too far,' Nell said, her face serious. 'I'm kidding. You're in a funny mood.'

'I'm a bit nervous, to be honest. I haven't had a great week.'

'Yeah, when you cancelled on Tuesday it made me pretty mad. Sorry if I was...I dunno, an arsehole.'

'It's okay.' Katie wanted to tell her she had been an arsehole and she had almost not come because she didn't want to be ridiculed again.

The waitress sat them along the wall. Nell immediately went for the bench seat facing the room, which left Katie with the flimsy looking cane chair.

'You're not vegan or anything are you?' Nell asked, looking at the menu.

'No, I had steak at the Royal Oak, remember?'

'Oh yeah.' A small smile came across Nell's face. *Maybe she's remembering touching my ass,* Katie thought, and felt her cheeks become hot.

'How's the library business?' Katie asked as their coffees arrived.

'That's hardly the most interesting question you could ask.'

Stunned, Katie tried to form a reply.

'I mean, I guess it's okay to start with the humdrum,' Nell said.

Katie frowned. 'Do you like your job?'

'I believe we need to look after people in our society. I believe we need to make spaces where young people can hang out that are free, and I think we should pay more for art.'

Katie nodded. 'Right.'

'Basically, I believe in the job, but most of the people in management are wankers.' Then Nell smiled again. She didn't do it often, but when she did, her smile made everything else in the room fade.

'Does that make it hard to stay there?'

'No, because one day everyone will think it's worthwhile looking after the people, and nurturing writers, and musicians, and self-righteous academic dickheads.' She took a sip of her coffee. 'And what happened with your work? You said you'd had a rough week?'

Katie went through the story from the beginning with Winthrop and Joshua. Nell listened without interrupting. Her face remained stern, serious, and she watched Katie carefully as she spoke.

'Have you looked for a new job yet?' Nell said.

'I spent about half an hour on it yesterday, but this close to Christmas there's hardly anyone advertising.'

'How long could you afford to be out of work?'

'That's a bit personal, isn't it?' Katie said.

'If it were me, I wouldn't stay there another minute. I would take my shit and leave. But I could only afford to be out of work about two weeks before things started getting tight.'

'I have three weeks of annual leave that would be paid out when I left, and then, I guess I could go a month before I'd have to get onto Centrelink or the bank of Mum.'

Nell made a noise in her throat and folded her arms.

'What's that supposed to mean?' Katie asked.

'Nothing. You do what's right for you.'

'But you think I should leave.'

'You can't stay. What if next time your boss decides he's not going to make it awkward for him and refuses to take the client?'

'He wouldn't.'

'You didn't think he'd take the customer's side over yours either. He still did it.'

'You're right. I'm scared he'll give me a bad reference.'

'I guess that's a risk you'll have to take. Try to leave without hurting his pride, and he might give you a good reference. But let's be honest, he's probably decided you can't take a joke or take things too seriously.'

They were all the words she'd heard a hundred times before. A couple of years ago, when she'd been fresh out of uni, Katie had been out in a bar in Brunswick Street with a couple of friends. Most of them were gay, but she had thought they wouldn't need to worry.

She had gone to the bar to buy a drink for the girl she was seeing at the time, Ava, a tall, willowy blonde who didn't give off a gay vibe to most people. A man next to her looked her over, sizing her up it seemed.

'You a dyke then?' he said, his speech slurred.

Katie said nothing, pretending she hadn't heard him.

He grabbed her shoulder 'Oi. I asked you a dyke?'

'Don't touch me please,' she said, her voice calm and firm.

'What you gonna do, butchy?'

'I'm trying to have a drink with my friends,' she said.

'You know what you lezzos need is a good dick up ya.'

The bartender had his back to them and wouldn't have heard over the loud music. She drew in a breath. 'You offering are ya, mate?'

'Nah, I wouldn't even rape a bitch like you. Not worth the effort.'

She turned away from the man as he wobbled on the bar stool. She walked as slowly as she dared back to her friends.

'We have to leave. Now.' She grabbed Ava's hand and pulled her out of her chair and towards the exit. Ava stared at her wide-eyed but seemed to understand now was not the time for questions.

When the group got to the street, the man at the bar had made his way to the front of the venue.

'He's following us. We need to get out of range.'

'What the fuck, Katie?'

'I'm sorry. He started saying some shit and of course I took the bait, didn't I?'

'Always one to poke the bear.' Ava's mouth set into a grim line.

'I'll feel better when we're away from here.'

Katie hailed a taxi and the two other women climbed in. As Katie was about to close the front passenger door the man caught up to them. He grabbed hold of the car door as she tried to pull it closed.

'Oi, bitch. You don't just walk away from me. It's fucking rude.'

'I don't want any trouble, mate.'

'Well you got trouble. Get out.'

Katie turned to the driver. 'Let's go, yeah?' The taxi driver started to move away down Brunswick Street, but the traffic meant they couldn't go very fast.

The drunk held onto the door for about twenty-five metres and then stumbled on the tram tracks. He fell and let go of the door. Katie slammed it closed. 'Lock the doors will you.'

'Sure, of course. You shouldn't encourage them, only makes them more mad,' the driver said.

'I don't need your input on it, thanks.' Katie turned to watch the street go by. The taxi ride was tensely silent.

Later that night, when she and Ava were snuggled into each other in Katie's bed, her anger returned.

'Un-fucking-believable,' Katie said.

'Try to let it go, babe.'

'What if I can't let it go? I can't live my life avoiding conflict. It'd find me even if I did.'

Ava sighed. 'You don't have to make yourself such a target though.'

It had been all she could do to stop herself from throwing Ava out of the bed right then. She had done nothing to invite harassment. It seemed just being herself made her a target. She could see answering back hadn't been a good choice, but too often someone made her feel like a freak for her short hair, and boxy, muscular body.

Katie shook her head clear of the memory and looked up at Nell.

'Where did you go?' Nell asked.

'Just remembering.'

'Some memory. You look like you might cry.'

How does she always say exactly the thing I don't want her to say? Katie thought as she swallowed, trying to push down the tears.

'Fine. Don't tell me.'

'It's not that.'

'Hey, it's fine. I hardly know you.' Nell looked at her watch. 'I better get going.'

'It's not that, I just...' but she didn't know why she didn't want to talk about it. It had been the point she'd stopped fighting back when men treated her like shit. She'd managed to tell Joshua about what Winthrop had done, after years of being dismissed or making things worse now she felt like it had exposed her in the workplace.

Katie felt like she had a sign on her forehead, 'not worth it.' She didn't know what to say to Nell. She put her off her ease so badly she marvelled they'd got through this long without Katie making a fool of herself.

'See you around.' Nell stood up and walked out of the café. Katie sat there, stunned, for some time before the waiter came to clear away their dishes.

'Did you want the bill now?' he asked.

'Oh, sure.'

How could she just storm off and leave me with the bill? For fuck's sake, she invited me on this date. She pursued me. I shouldn't have to get stuck paying for her.

Katie paid the bill, more than it was worth, and seethed as she walked the short distance back home.

When she got there, she found Sarah sitting on the veranda couch smoking a joint with her housemate.

'Hi,' Katie said.

'Hi,' Sarah replied.

'Smoke?' Raphael, her Columbian housemate, held out the spliff.

'Yeah, alright.' Katie sat on the edge of the veranda and the three of them smoked in silence until nothing remained but the roach.

Raphael was usually chatty, but he seemed to have realised the sisters didn't to want to talk.

'I'm never dating again,' Sarah said finally.

'Oh?' Katie said.

'Yeah. I'm just going to be alone.'

'What if you get horny?'

'I'll buy a good vibrator.'

'What happened to you then?' Katie hadn't seen her sister for a while and had started to think she'd done something to offend her.

'Ned told me not to date his friend Nick...'

'So you had to?'

'Hey! I did find Nick very attractive and something about the conflict between what Ned said and the way I felt with him made it more exciting.'

'And?'

'I kicked him out of bed and I'm pretty sure Ned's forgiven me.'

'I just had the date from hell,' Katie said.

'With the tattooed one from footy? Didn't you cancel on her?'

'Where did you hear that?'

'You told me,' Sarah said.

'Oh, yeah.' Katie giggled as the weed started to kick in. 'I convinced her to give it another try. Or maybe she convinced me...'

'What a pair we make.'

'You can say that again.'

'What a pair we make,' Sarah said laughing.

Once they finished laughing, and the cool breeze came over the veranda as the afternoon settled in, melancholy washed over Katie.

'You think we'll ever get it right?' she asked.

'Relationships? Nah, I told you I'm giving them up.'

'But didn't you want to have a family, and a dog and a farm...maybe not the farm.'

'Yeah. I thought being a mum was about the best thing a woman could do, but I'm not getting any younger.'

'You're only twenty-nine. You've got like, ten years still.'

Sarah shrugged. 'What do I want kids for except because it seemed like a good idea at the time? I mean Mum certainly didn't get much joy out of having us, except to torture Dad, and to criticise us all the time.'

'Yeah, and poor old Dad didn't have a great run of it. Only saw us on weekends. We hardly know him.'

'He could have seen us more. I think it suited him to stay in his little bungalow and watch life pass him by.'

'Funny how he never managed to stick with anyone after Mum ditched him.'

'Maybe he has some sort of arrangement.'

'Gross. I don't want to think of Dad having sex.'

'Some people have trouble with fidelity,' Sarah said.

'We've had our issues but that hasn't been one.'

'There are a lot of other ways a relationship can be fucked up.'

'True that.' Katie looked at the skies as the dark grey clouds scudded by.

29.

Appendicitis

Sarah had settled into a routine. She went to work, she came home, her housemates had finished classes, but they still spent most of their time in their rooms. She suspected they were watching television shows on their computers. The weeks crawled by but at least Sarah wasn't hurting.

Henry had stopped sending her offensive messages, and all the bills from the wedding were finally settled. It almost felt safe to pick up her phone again.

Sarah had shifts every day between Christmas and New Year's. Staff who had families and small children got first preference for time off during the holiday period. Although the elective surgeries stopped for most of December and January when the consultants took holidays, the hospital stayed busy with people coming through the Emergency Department.

Today one of her patients had a badly infected leg. He'd cut himself when he fell from the ladder putting up Christmas decorations ten days before and, because he was older, his wound hadn't healed. He'd waited until it had gone completely septic before going to the doctor, and the GP had sent him straight to the hospital.

Emergency surgery had removed all the necrotic flesh, now he had to stay in hospital until they were sure the infection hadn't got into his blood. A grumpy man in his late sixties who liked to use his buzzer. She tried not to resent him, he had a lot of pain, he couldn't go home for Christmas, and he couldn't move far without help, but sometimes she struggled.

She'd also had a woman, about her age, admitted earlier that morning, recovering from a burst appendix. She thought her abdominal pain was just related to her menstrual cycle, and she had to take herself to hospital when the small vestigial organ had split under the pressure of the infection.

'Hi Zoe, I'm Sarah, I'll be looking after you today.' Sarah read her name from the chart when she introduced herself.

'Hi,' Zoe replied, still groggy from surgery.

'Are you feeling alright?' Sarah felt her forehead for fever and clicked in the inner ear thermometer to check it; 37.6° C, on the high side but not far outside the normal range. Sarah made a note and checked the doctor's instructions; Zoe couldn't have any medications for another hour.

'I'm okay. I think.'

'Well, you don't need to do anything, just lie back and have a little sleep. You'll feel groggy after the anaesthetic. I'll wake you when it's time for your meds, and otherwise you just use this buzzer' —Sarah held up the remote which had the nurse call button and the controls for the T.V., — 'to get my attention.'

'Thanks.' Zoe laid her head back against the pillows and closed her eyes.

She looks pretty wrecked, Sarah thought. She replaced the medical chart in the basket attached to the end of the bed and went to check on the others on the ward. Ned started work in a couple of hours, and it was just her and the Nurse-in-Charge until then.

*   *   *

Ned arrived fifteen minutes late, sweaty and red-faced. 'Sorry, sorry.'

'What happened to you?' Sarah asked.

'The bloody bus broke down didn't it? I had to get out and wait for the next one, and then it was bloody packed.'

'Well you're here now. Deep breath.' She put her hand on his upper arm.

Ned went to put his bag in a locker and came back running his fingers through his hair.

'Who's in then?'

Sarah ran through the patients, and how they were doing today. When she got to Zoe, Ned stopped her.

'What's her name again?'

Sarah checked the list, 'Zoe Fraser.'

'I didn't know she was sick!'

'What do you mean? Why would you have known?'

'She's my friend. I was just around at her place a couple of days ago. How did she get from there to here so quickly?'

'Probably from pretending not to be in pain. Didn't want to make a fuss.'

'Maybe next time she'll know to make a fuss earlier.'

Because the doctors never send women away with abdominal pain saying it's just their period, or ovaries and to come back when there's a real problem, she thought. 'Yes, well, they took her appendix out, so she shouldn't have the same trouble again.' She smiled, but her attempt at a joke didn't get the reaction she hoped for. Ned shuffled his feet, lingering in the nurse's station.

'What?' she asked.

'I don't know whether I should tell you.'

'You have to tell me now.'

'Zoe is Nick's ex. The one he fucked over.'

'Oh,' Sarah said.

That's interesting, she thought. She's sick and probably doesn't want to rehash a break-up. I'll have to leave her to recover, at least until tomorrow, then I'll try to talk to her.

*　　*　　*

She went to check on Zoe on her way home.

'Ned told me you and Nick were... had...' Zoe said.

'He told you?'

'Yeah, I hope that's okay.'

'I guess.' Sarah looked at her feet, 'I wasn't going to say anything.'

'I don't mind. It's in the past now.'

'I know, but you're here trying to get well, and you don't need to be dragged back through drama.'

'It really wasn't as dramatic as Ned likes to make out.'

'Oh?' Sarah looked up, Zoe had put the bed up, so she could sit.

'Ned likes to play up how bad Nick is. I don't know why, maybe he's a little jealous.'

'Jealous?'

'Yeah, he had always fancied me, I knew he did, but I thought he meant no harm. When I got together with Nick he finally understood friends meant friends.'

Sarah's belly felt full of worms writhing around. Ned had shown a couple of times he wanted to take things with her further. Trying to make him understand his feelings weren't reciprocated had been one of the most awkward conversations she'd ever had.

He hadn't spoken to her for several weeks, and she had assumed he was too ashamed, or too hurt, to be her friend. She kept expecting to come into work and find Ned didn't work on her ward anymore. But eventually things went back to the way they had been before.

'I think you know what I mean,' Zoe said.

'Ned falls for people easily. No, that didn't come out right…I mean he feels things very intensely. It must be awful to love someone who doesn't love you back.'

'Twice.'

And to have Nick swoop in both times, she thought.

'You can ask you know, what happened with Nick and I,' Zoe said.

'Are you sure you're feeling up to it? I'm here tomorrow.'

'No, it's fine.' Zoe struggled to reposition the pillow. Sarah stepped forward and they wrestled it into a better position.

'So, what happened? Nick's version seemed a bit weird, if I'm honest.'

'It was weird. Nick's a free spirit. He's gorgeous and passionate, but you can't always count on him. Sometimes he gets caught up in something so intensely he'll forget to come home for hours, forgets you made arrangements. He would work himself to the point of

exhaustion campaigning or whatever, and then get mad
at me for telling him to take it easy.'

Sarah looked out the window, covered in old, dusty
rain spatters. The hospital stood on the top of a hill, and
the view stretched out over the roofs of the buildings
and down towards the public garden. She sighed. 'I
thought maybe if I could get interested in his causes, or
if I could somehow understand his obsession, then I'd
feel better about the whole thing.

'But by then he and I were in trouble. More than him
forgetting me; he didn't seem to be in love with me
anymore.

'I guess I was in denial, because I booked a flight to
follow him up to a protest in Queensland, and when I
told him he looked like I'd slapped him in the face.'

'What did he say?' Sarah asked.

'He said he was glad I was taking an interest, but it
wouldn't fix our relationship; we'd drifted apart. We
were very different. My family were a quiet
conservative Anglo household and his family are loud
and passionate Greeks. They do everything full bore,
but they're fickle.

'They seemed to welcome me into the family, but I
didn't know how to deal with them. I didn't know how
to love the parts of Nick that were loud and brash. He
said I loved with a version of him he couldn't be
anymore. He was dying trying to tone himself down for

me and he often forgot himself when he was away from me.'

'Jesus. Sounds devastating.'

'He told the truth. I did want to love him, but I wanted a sanitised version I could take home to my parents. I wanted him to fit into a neat box and trying to make that happen made us both miserable.' Zoe brushed her hands over her sheets, smoothing them, then flinched as she touched her wound.

'We split up on good terms. I went to Queensland on my own, and I had a fabulous time, but the split was really hard on me. It led to some real soul searching and I think all Ned sees is Nick seduced me and then broke my heart.' Zoe sighed.

'But you're still friends with Ned?'

'Yeah. He supported me during that time. He still has feelings for me I can't return, like he has for you. He's confused but he's a good friend most of the time '

Sarah rubbed her hands across her eyes. So much new information to process. Nick as a wild Adonis, untameable and passionate. He had many attractive characteristics, but she didn't want to make the same mistake Zoe made. She wouldn't be second best again

Perhaps Nick's passion would release something inside her, now she had to decide whether she could embrace her own wildness.

30.

East Brunswick Terrace

In the days after her unsuccessful date with Nell, Katie spent a lot of time thinking about everything she'd done wrong. If she had been more open, if she hadn't been offended. Nell couldn't know she had a history of people ignoring her protests.

She thought about Nell a lot. Her beautiful, angular face, her uneven hair, her skin, smooth and golden. She thought of Nell when she lay alone in bed and pleasured herself thinking of the ways she'd fuck Nell if she were there.

'I know we didn't end well last time, but would you be interested in trying one more time?' Katie sent a text message late in the evening a couple of days after their brunch.

'Let's do drinks tomorrow. After footy training.'

Friday night was usually a big one for Katie, after-training drinks were liable to get messy, and generally their games were on Sundays, so Saturday could be written off with a hangover without her feeling too guilty.

'Sounds good. See you there!'

Katie didn't know if Nell was bad news but thought she should give it another try. She hadn't had sex in a very long time.

*   *   *

Friday night at training Katie went hard. Joshua had been huffing around the clinic making a show of how uncomfortable he felt having her in the same room as him all day. She was angry and exhausted from holding all the tension.

Nell arrived towards the end of training, taking her usual spot up against the fence near the goal posts. She wore cut off black denim shorts and Katie saw her legs were also covered in flash tattoos.

How much more of her is inked? Katie wondered, mentally undressing Nell. The ball came towards her and Katie forced her mind back on the game.

Nell stayed at the fence until they had finished the warm down, watching them all, barely moving.

Katie showered, dressed and put on her shoes ready to go back outside the pavilion.

'Nell's loitering at the fence again. I thought you two flopped.' Cardo said, nudging her in the ribs.

'Gonna give it another go. She's really hot and I think it confuses me and I fuck up.'

'Go get it, girl!'

'Thanks.' Katie stood up and walked toward the door with as much confidence as she could muster.

Nell waited outside the pavilion as she came out, standing in the pool of shadow just outside the spread of the fluorescent lights under the veranda.

'Geez, I didn't see you there!' Katie said.

'I blend into the background.'

'Yeah, righto.'

Nell stuck her tongue out. 'You were good today. I dunno, you were more aggressive, or something.'

She felt her cheeks colouring at the compliment. She didn't want to be overly aggressive and certainly didn't want to be playing angry all the time. 'Thanks.'

'Where are we going?' Nell rolled a cigarette and lit it. 'Want one?'

'Nah, thanks. I don't have anywhere in mind.'

'I thought we could go to my place, I have beers.'

Katie took a step backwards. 'Oh, okay.'

She hadn't intended to go so fast, but perhaps they had better just get it out of the way. She'd never turned down anyone as hot as Nell.

*　　　*　　　*

Nell's place was in East Brunswick, an up and coming area with expensive renovated places and run-down share house hovels next to each other. She lived in a single-story terrace place, which shared walls with both neighbours. Some of the terraces were from the late nineteenth and early twentieth century, but the brown bricks and white metal work over the front window seemed more 1950s to Katie.

The door was on the left, and the front window obviously a bedroom. Nell opened the door into a dark hallway. A second bedroom sat behind the first, Katie couldn't work out where the light would come in from, there was no visible window. Further in, past the second bedroom came the lounge and then the kitchen. These two rooms were slightly narrower than the bedrooms and the windows looked out onto the brick wall of the neighbouring house.

'Beer?' Nell asked.

'Yeah. What have you got?'

'I have Furphies. Or Coopers, but that's stout.'

'I'd better take a Furphy then.'

Nell pulled two beers from the fridge. 'Let's drink in the garden.'

Katie followed her out into a tiny brick-paved courtyard. There were plants hanging in rows from trellises attached to the walls. Two spindly metal chairs and a matching table sat covered in old cigarettes and tiny leaves from the tea tree hanging over the fence.

The summer evening was humid and warm, and the smell of rain hung in the air. 'Looks like it might storm.'

'I love thunderstorms. They get me all worked up,' Nell said, with a wriggle of her eyebrows.

Katie drank her beer quickly for courage. She'd never been this jumpy before, with some alcohol under her belt hopefully the throwaway dismissive comments would roll off her back.

Nell took her time with hers. 'You need another one?' she said, looking at Katie's empty bottle.

'I can wait till you're ready.'

'It's cool.' She went back into the kitchen for another Furphy.

'I've been thinking about you a lot. I'm glad you sent me a message,' Nell said.

'Yeah, I didn't want to leave things on a sour note.'

'I don't usually give people second chances, let alone thirds.'

Katie frowned. *What does she mean by that?* 'I appreciate it.'

Nell took a long swig of her beer and said nothing. To fill in the silence, Katie started talking about her day at work.

'You're still working for the fascist?'

'He's not that bad,' Katie said.

'If you say so.'

'Let's not talk shop. Who's the gardener?'

'Me. I love to have green things around me, but they won't grow inside, not enough sun.' Nell kept the conversation going on this track until they'd both finished their beer.

'Let's go back inside.' Nell stood up.

'Okay.'

Nell dropped the empty beers into the recycling bin with a crash. She took Katie's hand and led her into the second bedroom. Instead of flicking on the overhead light, she turned on fairy lights which ran around the picture rail a couple of feet below the ceiling. They were red and bathed the bedroom in a lurid glow.

Nell closed the door and pushed Katie backwards onto the bed. She kissed her hard on the mouth, her small limbs contained surprising strength. Katie hadn't been ready for the pounce, but the alcohol and the sensation of Nell's plump, soft lips on hers brought arousal flooding forward.

They spent the next few hours taking turns pleasuring each other. Katie had been worried she'd forgotten how, but Nell's writhing limbs and throaty calls of appreciation told her she had nothing to worry about.

Katie hadn't been touched for so long she felt her emotions running wild inside her; one moment she was giggling with pleasure, then after one particularly strong orgasm she felt a few tears slip from her eyes.

Discovering the Franklins

When they had both had their fill they lay back, quiet. Eventually Katie fell asleep, naked and sweaty under the red glow.

*   *   *

In the morning, light came in through an uncovered skylight above them. Katie looked at her watch; not yet six a.m. She was tired and bleary from beer and sex. She looked over at Nell still sleeping; apparently used to the light flooding in from the ceiling.

She quietly extracted herself and slipped on her jeans and T-shirt before heading out to find the toilet.

As Katie tiptoed towards the bathroom, the front door opened.

'Hi Meg, I didn't know you were back,' he said.

'Uh,' Katie began. As the man in front of her stepped into the house his eyes adjusted to the gloom; clearly, he'd mistaken her for someone else.

'Oh, I... never mind,' he said, opening the front bedroom door and diving into it. Katie wondered who Meg was, and why he thought she would be her.

When she came back from the bathroom Nell slept soundly, her mouth hanging open and her arms and legs sprawled across the mattress.

Katie took her jeans off but left her knickers and T-shirt on. She lay on the bed, which smelled of sex, beer and cigarettes. She was determined not to fall asleep again, she wanted to ask about Meg, but when she woke up to Nell sliding her hand up under her T-shirt, she realised she'd drifted off.

'Good morning,' Nell whispered.

'Hi.' Katie stiffened. Nell's hand stilled, before pulling away.

'What's wrong?'

'Who's Meg?'

'Where did you hear that?' Nell asked.

'It doesn't matter, answer the question.'

Nell hesitated. 'She's my girlfriend.'

Fuck, Katie thought. I knew something felt off and I ignored it. 'Your girlfriend?'

'Yes. She does fly in fly out work on mines in W.A. She's away most of the time.'

'I see.' Katie slowed her breathing, trying to keep her anger down.

'I didn't think it would be a problem.'

'No, the girlfriend you didn't tell me about, why would that be a problem?'

'Come on. We hadn't ever talked about exclusivity.'

'No, but when I'm pursued by someone, I assume they're not already in a relationship.'

'My girlfriend doesn't understand me like you do—'

'Are you fucking serious? That's straight from cheaters handbook.' Katie got out of the bed and shoved her feet into her jeans so roughly she stumbled.

'I thought we were having fun.' Nell lay propped up on one elbow, her face calm with a hint of a smile.

'You don't understand people, do you? Most of us don't like being lied to.'

Katie picked up her shoes and bag and stormed out of the house. She slammed the front door behind her and it made a satisfying crash into the empty morning. She walked down the street until she turned a corner and found a low brick fence she could sit on to put on her shoes.

The sex had been mind-blowing, but this feeling of emptiness she'd hoped she'd left behind.

How come Cardo didn't warn me off? She thought. *I'm going to have to have a word with her.* She shoved her feet into her shoes and marched off towards home.

31.

The Blind Leading the Blind

Katie had Cardo's number, and she was about to call
her to have it out with her when she remembered the
time. Her head ached from the beer and lack of sleep.

It's no good blaming Cardo. Hiding a girlfriend,
letting me pursue her. The nerve, the sheer balls on her!
Katie thought as she stomped all the way home. Not far,
only about twenty-five minutes' walk, and the exercise
got some of the adrenaline out of her system.

In the lesbian community, even in a city as big as
Melbourne, people knew each other. Nell would soon
get a reputation and burn every connection she had.

Katie couldn't imagine being away from the woman
she loved for weeks at a time. Mines were big money,
but apart from the obvious detriment caused to the
environment, especially with open pits, the social
isolation didn't appeal and there seemed to be quite a
lot of injuries. Some were caused by the nature of the
work, and some were caused by the fact the crews out

there were bored, lonely and had access to plenty of alcohol.

By the time she arrived home, she didn't feel so much like murdering anyone. She was still angry at Cardo, but given Nell hid things, it made more sense Cardo hadn't known.

Everyone was still asleep in her house, and despite being tired, Katie didn't feel like going back to bed.

She looked over the shelves in the kitchen; there were some tortillas, some salsa, eggs of unknown age. In the fridge, she found an avocado, cheese and some bacon.

Seems like breakfast burritos are on the menu, she thought. After the walk home, her appetite had hit her hard; her belly groaned and gurgled. She'd run out of coffee grounds, but her Columbian housemate never let his supply run dry.

She had been cooking for about ten minutes, long enough for the bacon to be half way done and the eggs to go into the pan when Raphael came into the kitchen.

'Do you need breakfast?' she asked.

'Of course. If you are cooking, I am eating. Thank you.'

They ate on the veranda. They had a table and chairs in the back yard, but at that time of the morning it was far too sunny for Katie. She didn't want to take a pain-killer, she thought she deserved the hangover as a reminder not to trust hot tattooed women who were cut of her league.

'Tell me about your night. You do not look happy.' Raphael said, his burrito slowly dripping salsa onto his plate.

'Obvious, it is?'

'Yes.'

Katie told him the story, her own burrito getting cold as she did so.

'You are better than this *puta.*'

'That's sweet of you say,' she said, cringing at the term. Nell could be called many things but that gave whores a bad name. She took a bite of burrito before she could say anything else.

Raphael finished his food and sipped his coffee while telling her about his evening. He'd been out at the Peel, a well-known gay bar in Collingwood. His Latino good looks and youth were always in demand. It didn't hurt he spent a lot of time in the gym.

Katie was a surprised he'd gotten up so early. When she looked closely, she saw he still had remnants of glitter around his eyes and in his hair. *He hasn't been to bed yet,* she thought.

Even with the coffee, the food had made her sleepy. She got up, put her dishes on the sink for later, and crawled into bed. She hadn't showered and smelled of sex, and she hadn't cleaned her teeth, but sleep pressed down on her.

*   *   *

Katie woke to the sound of her phone ringing.

If it's her, I'm not answering, she thought.

'Hi Sarah?' Katie's voice croaked.

'Oh shit, sorry, I thought you'd be up by now.'

'What's the time?'

'Nearly twelve.'

'Oh. I should be awake.'

Silence filled the line. Katie rubbed her free hand across her eyes. 'Did you call for something in particular?'

'I, well, I want you to convince me not to see Nick again.'

'I thought you said he was shifty. Why are you even considering it?

'I did. I... have new information,' Sarah said.

'It doesn't change the fact he's a twat. Just be single for a while.'

Sarah sighed. 'Yes, well, I could do that, I suppose. It's just he's a really good lover, and I think he deserves another chance.'

'Either you're just horny thinking you can do a no strings arrangement, which we both know you can't, or this new info changes everything.'

'I met his ex.'

'Bullshit.' Katie felt wide awake now.

Sarah told her the whole story, including Ethel's death alone in a hospital ward.

'Jesus. The universe has been laying it on thick for you.' Katie didn't believe in fate or predetermination, neither did Sarah, but sometimes it seemed as though the signs were too obvious to ignore.

'But the ex, she doesn't hate him. If he'd done what Ned said, then surely, she'd be more bitter than that, wouldn't she?' Sarah said.

'You call me and say 'tell me not to do this thing' but it's clear what you want is for me to give you permission. You're asking the wrong person, sister.'

'What do you mean?'

'I'm no relationships expert, Sarah. I can't even get as far as living together, so you really should do what you think is right.'

'Yeah, but what if I choose wrong again? I don't want to spend a few years of my life fitting in with someone else, becoming the perfect girlfriend and forgetting who I am again only to find out I've been an idiot and be in the same position I'm in now?'

'Most relationships end. It's a statistical fact. But there are fun times and joy to be gained out of it too. The fact you break up after a year, or three years, or ten years doesn't automatically make it a failure.'

Geez, Katie, get off the bandwagon. She doesn't need a lecture, she just wants to tell you her news and then go and do what she's gonna do anyway, Katie thought.

'Shit. That's pretty deep. Where did you get that?'

'I dunno, probably Oprah or something.'

'You have never once watched Oprah.' Sarah laughed.

'You don't know what I have and haven't watched.' She had intended it to be banter, a joking reply to her sister's light-hearted teasing, but her tone come out too sharp.

'Sorry.'

'No, I'm sorry. It's not you.' She told her sister what happened with Nell. This time it she had to hold her tears back a couple of times.

'It really, really sucks when you've had some good sex and then they go and fuck it up by being dick bags. Remember Cameron from work?'

'Doctor type? Good face?'

'Yeah. I took him home after the Christmas party.'

'Isn't he married?'

'Yep. Told me they were separated. And gullible Muggins over here believed him.'

'What a fuck-face,' Katie said. She looked at the closed curtains in her bedroom, the day outside was obviously bright and beautiful behind the fabric.

'Well we certainly know how to pick 'em, don't we?' Sarah said.

'Yep. We had some great role models to learn from.'

Katie remembered the fights she'd watched her parents have, especially when their dad tried to bring his girlfriends along to family gatherings. Once he'd sent his girlfriend of the time to pick up the girls because a retaining wall had collapsed and he had to stay late at work to fix it. Their mum was furious and had refused to let the girlfriend into the house. She'd sat outside in the car for nearly two hours until Graham turned up to take them.

The two sisters had also been party to the fight between Graham and the girlfriend about why he hadn't defended her with his ex-wife, saying he was ashamed of her and still in love with Hannah, she would always come second to his kids and his ex.

He didn't have anything to defend himself from that claim, Graham loved his kids, and Katie understood, as an adult, how difficult it would have been to keep in Hannah's good books to make sure he saw them. She was hurt by his cheating and she made him pay for it over and over and over.

Their mother was vindictive, and their father did nothing to stop her. Unsurprisingly they had grown up to make terrible relationship choices.

'The blind leading the blind, eh?' Sarah said, dragging Katie back to the reality lying in bed at midday, sweating under the bedclothes.

'You may as well see where this thing goes with Nick. Yeah, you might get hurt, but what if he's the one for you and you let him go? I know I'd rather regret things I did than things I didn't.'

'Sounds like you got that from a cheap pack of tarot cards.'

'Those cards were very expensive.'

Sarah laughed. 'I can't seem to get Nick out of my head, and now there isn't really a good reason not to go for it. I mean, it's not just wishful thinking?'

Katie sighed, as much as she loved her sister, she really needed to learn to make decisions on her own. After the trauma of cancelling her wedding she had lost a lot of confidence in herself.

Deep breath, just tell her it'll be alright and then you can get on with doing something useful with your day, like balling out Cardo.

'It'll be fine. If you're still thinking about him then you have to give it a try. You've got this.'

'Thank you. I better go. I'll see you at Dad's tomorrow night yeah?'

Shit, I forgot about that, she thought. 'Yep, see you there.'

32.

Sorry is the Hardest Word

Sarah stared at her phone and couldn't bring herself to call him. What if he didn't want to hear from her? What if he had lost interest?

I'll have some dinner and then I'll call. But then it might be too late, and he might think I'm really rude. She thought herself in circles.

She slapped herself lightly across the cheeks to psych herself up. The phone rang and rang. She subconsciously counted them. After twenty-nine rings, the line dropped out. He didn't have voicemail.

She tried him a few more times, early, middle of the day, evening, and each time the phone just rang out. He was active on Facebook, commenting on friends' photos and posting a link to a Kickstarter campaign.

What can I say to him in a text that will convey how sorry I am for being a total weirdo? For taking Ned's word over his, for ignoring the great time we had in each other's company.

She wrote out the message to him over twenty times. It never seemed quite right, and she worried it would get sent accidentally before she'd perfected it.

Her next shift at work wasn't until Wednesday, and she had far too much time on her hands. Time she spent thinking about reasons for Nick to be angry with her, to not care for her, to have already moved on to another woman.

The dinner at Dad's on Sunday had been uneventful. She wanted to talk to Katie about Nick, and to talk over the shit Nell pulled, but not in front of Graham.

She wanted to invite Ned out for a coffee or lunch, but she had the feeling he wouldn't want to hear about her and Nick. She didn't want to acknowledge her best friend was at not exactly impartial and possibly in love with her.

Without Ned, she didn't have many friends to call on. The friends she'd had with Henry were his friends, or couples where the guy was his friend; she had to be friends with the woman by default. They were polite enough when she cancelled the wedding, but none of them had reached out to her since then. They had chosen to stay with Henry and that left her just about on her own.

She decided to head down to CERES just in case Nick was working in his aunt's plot. She couldn't figure out what to say in a message and he didn't seem to be answering her calls, so she'd have to find him in person.

Sunny and clear, the temperature was in the high twenties, pleasantly warm. Sarah rode her bike there, pulling a battered hat out of her bag and shoving it on her head as soon as she arrived.

She walked around CERES, taking in the noticeboard on the side of the train, looking for anyone she knew hanging out in the café.

She had been around the train carriage three times checking the notice boards, she was procrastinating. By now the sun had slid down a little and blinded her as she walked up the slope.

'Sarah!'

She recognised his voice before she saw him. She put up her hand to shield her eyes. 'Hi Nick. I hoped I would find you here.'

Nick wore overalls without a shirt, the same as the day she had first met him. His dark eyes were shaded by his ratty straw hat. He knelt in the dirt planting seedlings.

'It's probably too late in the season, but I'm going to give them a try,' he said.

'I hope your aunt appreciates the time you're putting into this.'

'Well, I'm staying with her, and she's feeding me, so I feel like I have to contribute.'

'Of course.' Sarah looked at the neat rows, she didn't know what the plants were.

'So, uh, how have you been?' Nick asked, after a long period of silence.

'I've been better.' She wanted to kiss him so much she felt dizzy.

'Yeah.'

'I met Zoe.'

'And you're still talking to me?' He laughed, a little tinge of sadness entered his eyes.

'I've been trying to call you.'

'Sorry. My phone's busted. I cropped it one too many times, and I'm feeling pretty free not having it glued to my hip all the time.'

He didn't know she'd been calling. If she left now she wouldn't have to admit what a fool she'd been to take Ned's advice. She would be lonely, but there would be other men out there for her. He bent to makes small a hole in the dirt with his finger and delicately deposited the seedling into it.

'I'm so sorry, Nick. Ned told me a bunch of stuff and I know you told me it wasn't true, but I didn't want to be hurt again. I believed him.' She took a breath.

'And then I met Zoe, the woman whose life you apparently destroyed, and she was so nice about you, even after you'd broken up, she said Ned had fallen in love with her, and probably me as well.

'I've never been good at relationships, or friendships it turns out, and I didn't want to lose my best friend because he's a jackass, but on the other hand, you don't deserve to be thrown away like that,' she said.

Nick remained still, kneeling in the dirt in front of her, his head bent down over his hands. 'What are you saying, Sarah?'

'Forgive me for the other morning. I'm asking you if you still like me. I'm asking if you want to go on a date with me.'

Nick took off his hat and rubbed his muscular forearm over his brow. He put his hat back on before he answered. 'I appreciate how hard it must have been for you to come and say all those things to me. I'm flattered, obviously.'

He's going to say no. Oh fuck, he's going to say no and I'm going to be humiliated again. She started to breathe faster.

'It's hard for me to be really open to this when I get such mixed signals from you,' he said.

'I understand.'

'First you seem keen, then you don't contact me, then you invite me over for a drunken booty call, which I shut down because it's never a good idea, and then when we made love in the morning I thought we were starting something beautiful, but you just threw me out. How can I feel comfortable with you?'

'I know what I feel now. I know what I want.'

'I'm glad, I really am...'

'But?'

'But I can't say yes. I need to really process the changes of mood you've been through, I need to think about my priorities, what I'm doing in the next six months. I mean, I might not even be staying in Melbourne much longer.'

'Oh. I ...' she stuttered.

'You assumed. I understand. People assume I'm flighty and carefree, but I think everything through, especially if it's important.'

'You should. I'm sorry for springing it on you like this.'

'It was very nice to see you, Sarah.'

It felt like a brush-off.

'Is there anything I can do to reassure you?' she asked.

'I just need to think it over. On my own.'

'I guess I'll wait to hear from you.'

'Yeah, I'll message you on Facebook. I'm probably not going to get a new phone for a while. It's all well and good to stay with relatives, costs are low, but when you're between jobs even low costs add up.'

'I hope to see you soon, then,' she said.

He waved from his position on the ground as she turned to go. He didn't offer her a hug or even a

handshake. She hadn't counted on him being so cold.
All she wanted to do was cry, but she couldn't weep in
public.

*   *   *

As soon as she got into her house Sarah ran up the
stairs and locked herself in the bathroom. The warm
day and riding hard all the way home had made her
sweaty and hot. When she was sad, she liked to run
herself a bubble bath, listen to sad music and cry.

She made the water cool, but not too cold, and put
her phone on the counter, playing her favourite sad
playlist. As she peeled away her clothes she could feel
the sadness releasing itself.

She set the playlist to random, and as she slipped
into the water, careful not to slosh too much over the
edges, it played *Mad World*; all she needed to break the
dam.

She wept in the bubbles until she became calm,
breathing in the lavender scent. The water was tepid,
but in the hot upstairs bathroom it didn't need to be
very hot. She put her head back on a rolled-up towel
and closed her eyes.

*   *   *

The water was quite cool when she woke. She
stretched her cold limbs and climbed out of the water.

She dried herself off, applied moisturiser, and picked
up her phone. She saw she had a message from Nick.

Her heart started pounding, if he'd decided he couldn't even try, she would cry again, but what if he wanted to give it a try? If he'd managed to forgive her poor decision making and wanted to be with her anyway?

Her hands were shaking and pruney as she slid her thumb over the notification.

'I'm sorry about today. I spent a lot of time telling myself I couldn't be in love with you. That you had made it clear you didn't want anything to do with me. When you were standing there saying you wanted me, I thought it must be a fresh way for Ned to make me hate myself.

'But then you walked away, and you seemed so sad. I thought to myself, what if this is real? Would I put my plans on hold to see where this leads? And I said to myself, she's worth giving it a try. So. I guess I'm saying yes to your date. If you'll have me.' He'd signed it with a kissy face emoji.

She reached out to grab the top of the sink to keep her wobbling legs under her. She ran into her bedroom and flung herself on the bed. It didn't seem real. She couldn't have hoped for a better outcome.

'How about I take you out to dinner. Tomorrow okay?' she sent back.

She saw the bouncing dots showing he was typing almost immediately.

'I'll see you tomorrow then.'

Sarah smiled and kissed her phone.

33.

Don't look back

Katie looked at her phone, for the seventh time in an hour. Nothing. She had been applying for lots of jobs, but this time of year no one seemed to be getting back to her. There were few jobs, and even fewer she wanted.

Why did Josh have to be such a gutless wonder? I liked that job, she thought.

She'd sworn off dating, for the moment at least. There was nothing worse that being the subject of gossip and the story about Nell had gotten around the footy club already. Most of the others were in long term relationships, and stories like what happened between her and Nell were discussed openly. Sometimes they talked about one topic for weeks, other times it was usurped quickly by another scandal.

Too bad for Katie it was a slow news month. Her phone buzzed, she picked it up without looking at the number.

'Hello Katie speaking?'

'It's Josh.'

Why didn't I look at the caller ID?

'Hi,' she said. She wouldn't give him any more of her time than was absolutely necessary. 'What do you want?'

'I wanted to see how you were doing.'

They had barely spoken since she told him to look for a new physio and Janet had arranged it so that all her clients were given to other therapists. She hadn't even been into the office for two weeks.

'Fine.' Katie tapped her fingers on the wooden coffee table.

'There are a couple of your things here at the clinic. Can you come by to get them?'

'What are they?' I'm not going unless they're important.

'There's a photo of your family, and some stuff we found in the kitchen. It would be best if you came in to collect them.'

'I'll see you later today.'

When she hung up the phone she swore. The nerve of him. Why couldn't he just post them, or get Janet to bring them to her house? They had her address.

She slipped out of her pyjamas and into her favourite jeans, and a plain blue T-shirt.

*   *   *

The clinic looked exactly the same as it always did. She took a deep breath and pulled open the front door. The first thing she noticed was that it was not Janet sitting behind the reception desk.

'Hi. I'm Katie. I used to work here, Josh said I had some things to collect.'

The new receptionist was very young looking, couldn't have been much more than eighteen, with strawberry blonde hair swept into a high, tight ponytail. She was wearing a garish orange dress, which was much too tight for a workplace, and her nails were fluorescent lime green. Where had she came from?

'I'm Natalia, I started last week. I'll have to get Josh to come see you. I don't know what stuff he meant for you to take. Give me a moment.' She flicked her ponytail and pressed the button to dial Josh.

'He'll be right out,' she announced.

I don't want to see him, Katie thought. She took a seat on one of the grey fabric chairs in the reception area and tried not to seethe.

'Katie. Thanks for coming.' Josh spoke softly, he seemed tired.

She stood and didn't shake his outstretched hand. He let his drop back by his side.

'Come into the kitchen,' he said.

'I don't have long.'

'I just need a minute.'

Katie rolled her eyes and followed him into the kitchen. There was a box sitting on the corner of the bench. It seemed very small and she wished she hadn't bothered to come.

'Have a seat,' Josh said. He barely made eye contact and seemed very ill-at-ease.

'I'll stand. As I said, I don't have long.'

'Let me come right down to it.' He took a deep breath, Katie's impatience built and she folded her arms across her chest. 'I need you back.'

'You need me back?' she said.

'The clinic hasn't been the same since you left. You were holding everyone together. Janet has stormed off in protest to the way she says I've treated you. I know she'd come back if you did, so I need you to come back to work.'

Katie thought of her withering bank account, it would be nice not to have to scrimp on things, or trawl through job ads, but then she remembered what Josh had been like. 'What's in it for me?'

'What do you mean?' He frowned.

'Well, after the stunt you pulled I said to myself I'd never come back here. So, I want you to explain to me why it's in my best interest to come back.'

'I told you, I need you here.'

'I heard you, but that doesn't mean anything to me. I don't need you. There are plenty of other jobs out there.' She lied.

'Uhh...' he stuttered. 'I paid you alright didn't I? We had some good times?'

'I can get paid anywhere, Josh. Why should I come back to you?'

Josh looked pale. His eyes darted around the room as though he was trying to come up with a good reason for her to come back behind the teabags. 'Because I want you here?'

'That's not good enough. You won't change. You haven't given me a single reason to come back that makes any difference.' She paused, hoping that he might suddenly see the foolishness of the way he was behaving. He said nothing, so she went on.

'That's my stuff, I presume?' She pointed to the small box in the corner.

'Yes.'

'Right. I'll be off then.' She strode over to the bench, picked up the box, which contained a small framed photo of her, Sarah and their Dad, and a blue and purple travel coffee mug.

I didn't need to come back for these. He just needed an excuse. He's not coping with the changes but they have nothing to do with me. If he'd learned anything from the situation then I might have been tempted to return, but nothing's changed.

'Goodbye Josh.'

Josh looked at her, his face seemed heavily lined in defeat, and said nothing. She turned away and walked out of the clinic without a backwards glance.

*   *   *

The next morning, Katie had a call from a recruiter she'd put her resume in to weeks before. It was a maternity leave cover, six-months contract, but Katie was confident that by then they would see she was a valuable employee and make sure to keep her.

34.

Meeting the family

Sarah and Nick went out for dinner the night after their text conversation in the bath. They had spent just about every night together since, always at Sarah's house.

She turned over on Saturday morning, and looked at him. She could tell he was awake, his breathing was not the slow, deep breathing of sleep.

'Why don't we ever hang out at your house?'

'Well, you know I'm living with my aunt. I didn't want to subject you to the full interrogation of my family so soon in the relationship.' His eyes were open, staring at the ceiling.

She sat up on one elbow, her brows drawn together in a frown. 'Are you worried about it?' She gave a little laugh.

'Yes.' He turned to her, his eyes swimming with concern.

'I'm not a delicate flower who needs protecting.'

'You may not be, but I am a little nervous. If Vicky doesn't like you, then I don't know how I'll live that down.'

She put her hand on his chest and ran her fingers over the dark curly hair. 'Does she often disapprove of people?'

'Yes. Frequently. Every woman I've ever introduced her to, she's found something wrong with.'

'Oh.' How would she get over this psychological barrier? It was clear that Nick couldn't fully relax into the relationship with his Aunt's disapproval hanging over them, but should she push him?

'There's nothing for it then,' she said.

'What do you mean?'

'Either we go through the Aunt gauntlet today, or we may as well end it now.' She smiled at him, hoping he would understand she was joking.

'This is serious, Sarah.' He frowned.

'I know it is, but the longer we avoid it, the more weight it will carry. It's like a Band-Aid. We just have to rip it off.'

He smiled, but the concern stayed in his eyes. 'Alright. We'll go today. You're not working are you?'

'No, I don't have a shift until tomorrow afternoon.'

'My aunt is preserving olives today. You'll have to help.'

'I know nothing about olives, but let's do it.' She leaned down to kiss him, his stubble tickled her skin in a way that was now familiar. She moved her hand down his chest, under the sheet towards his groin. 'Maybe we could go in a little while…'

He took her face in his hands and kissed her. 'You drive a hard bargain.'

*　　　*　　　*

Nick's aunt lived in West Brunswick. In front of the house was a small garden that was completely overrun with enormous tomatoes and beans on trellises. The front door was not locked, and Nick led her by the hand into the house.

'Yassou Vicky. Only me!' Nick called through the house. His aunt was in the kitchen at the back of the house, in standard terrace fashion the bedrooms were to the left and right of the central hallway, and the kitchen and dining room were at the back of the house. It was quite dark in the hallway and Sarah suddenly felt anxious. It had seemed like such a good idea that morning, when she was sleepy and happy, but now her palms were sweaty.

'Darling! Where have you been? I missed you.' A woman's voice called back from the kitchen.

As they stepped out of the dark hallway into the kitchen Sarah was almost blinded, the whole back of the house seemed to have been converted into a sunroom, the kitchen was covered in pale pine panelling and there was an enormous six burner stove taking up one wall. A tall, stout woman was standing at the island bench with a huge pot filled with brine, ladling it onto jars of green olives.

'I've brought someone to meet you.' Nick's voice wobbled a little. A week ago Sarah wouldn't have caught it, but now she knew more of his nuances.

'This is the girl you've been wasting your time with?' Vicky looked at Sarah as though she were food she didn't trust. She ran her eyes over her then nodded. 'She's too thin, and she'll never get babies through those hips.'

'Auntie, that's not very nice.' Nick's cheeks reddened.

'It's okay. I am very slim in the hips. I got it from my Dad's side.'

'Can you cook?'

'Well enough not to starve, but I'd love to learn.' Sarah clasped her hands in front of her and tried not to wring them. Vicky was even more severe than she'd anticipated.

The older woman stared at her, frowning for another few moments, then grinned broadly. 'We will teach you. Come here.' She gestured her around the bench. 'You, boy, go out into the garden and finish washing the other olives.'

'Yes, Auntie.' Nick flashed a grin at her and the tension in his shoulders seemed to have drained away when Vicky smiled.

'He's a very silly boy you know. Brought all these useless, cocky, no-good girls to meet me. You're the first one I have liked, you respect your elders but had enough backbone to stand up for yourself. You will be good for him. Now, you take this. Don't spill any.'

Sarah took the enormous spoon from her and started filling the jars with brine. Nick came in and out a few times, and Vicky barked orders at him, always with a wink to Sarah as she did.

This is how she shows him love, she thought. As she realised she had been drawn to Vicky's side in this game, she knew she'd been given the stamp of approval.